Metanoia

Other works by this author:

Final Flight of the Ranegr
The Starlight Lancer
The Awakening
Path of a Hero
The Cursed Jewel
The Star Warriors

Find them online at
https://www.cscooper.com.au/books

Metanoia

C. S. Cooper

For my siblings, nieces, and nephews.

CONTENTS

Metanoia

Acknowledgements

I acknowledge the artist group, CLAMP, whose manga inspired this story. I also thank the people who read my novel, *Final Flight of the Ranegr*. Since you were so intrigued by *The AXOM Saga*, and requested paperback copies, here you go. Then, there are my parents and family, who encouraged me to publish it.

The Story So Far

As seasons change, the seeds grow to bloom. Yet, only the strongest and hardiest flowers survive adversity, those becoming the most beloved of all.

A year ago, the life of Tokyo middle-schooler, Sakura Kinomoto, was an average one, and she loved every second of it. She had her best friend, Tomoyo Daidouji, her Dad, Franklin, and her older brother, Touya. Touya's best friend, Yukito Tsukishiro, often spent time with the family, and Sakura was absolutely smitten with him.

That all changed when Sakura discovered the magical Clow Cards. She unintentionally awakened them, and they scattered across the city. The Guardian of the Clow, Kerberus, bestowed upon her the Shadow Key, which she could use to find and seal away the Cards before they caused a tremendous calamity.

Along for the ride was Tomoyo, who recorded her exploits capturing the Clow Cards and uploaded them to the Internet. This made them instantly famous, and served as a perfect cover for their true activities. Seriously, who would've thought that videos about magic entities would be anything but CGI?

It did, however, incur the wrath of Xiaolang Lee, a descendent of the Clow Cards' creator. He declared Sakura an unfit Master of the Clow, and demanded she return the Cards to him. But when he later saw she could be a good

Master, he decided to train her in magic.

Lee wasn't the only one Sakura impressed. Upon obtaining all the Cards, Yukito revealed himself as the alter ego of Yue, Kerberus' counterpart. Yue carried out the Final Judgement on Sakura, in which she proved herself worthy. Yue reluctantly announced Sakura as the Master of the Clow, to the joy of Tomoyo and Kerberus. Even Lee was happy, having confided in Tomoyo that he'd always had feelings for Sakura.

Having averted the calamity of the Clow Cards, Sakura excitedly looked forward to her future of endlessly viral videos and magical hijinks!

Behind the veil of the cosmos, agents unknown and ancient extend their feelers and antennae, across space and time, searching … fearing … hunting …

1 | The New Semester

Twilight air trickled through the half-open window. It carried the warm scent of the last few days of summer. In the centre of Tokyo, you'd often smell the fumes of cars and hear the dull roar of traffic. But out in the suburbs, you can really enjoy the peace.

Sakura Kinomoto drew deep of the draught from the window. She ran her hands through her neck-length chestnut hair and yawned triumphantly.

"All done!" she sighed. She gazed over at the TV in her bedroom, in front of which a winged teddy bear pounded a fluorescent-red game controller frantically. A normal person would freak out at the sight of an animate teddy bear playing *Super Mario Odyssey*; even more so if that bear said, "Finally got ya homework done, eh?" with a thick Kansai accent.

Sakura was hardly normal, being a magic girl and all.

She plopped on her bed and stretched out. "Yep, the homework is out of the way. In your face, Brother Touya!"

"Ya shouldn't be like that," said the bear as he launched Mario over a horde of angry goombas. "Ya know, if he hadn't bet ya them chores, ya'd prob'ly be just findin' all that homework not done yet."

Sakura pursed her lips and glared at the living plush toy.

"I would have gotten it done faster if you'd helped out

instead of playing my games, Kero," she said.

"Games trump homework," said Kero. Then his large ears perked with excitement. "Since you're finished, I can do this." He quickly saved his game, closed the software and exchanged the cartridge for another game. Then, his body started to glow. It grew and grew, until he was the size of a lion.

Kero's larger form flexed his prehensile fingers and grinned. Then, he dexterously assembled the two controllers of Sakura's Nintendo Switch and began playing *Legend of Zelda*.

"I'mma get that *Lynel* now!" he growled excitedly.

Once again, a normal person would have freaked out.

Sakura just rolled her eyes at her guardian's video game addiction. Before she could make any comments, a pink, ornate book floated from her desk. The front cover, bearing the title 'The Clow,' glimmered in the late afternoon sun, and opened to reveal the large Cards concealed therein. Sakura gazed at the Cards.

She heard their voices in her mind, "We were glad to help with your studies, Master."

"Thanks, guys," said Sakura with a smile. She eyed the two labelled 'Sword' and 'Shield', and added, "You two were especially helpful with my math drills." She looked to the Cards bearing the images of various elemental nymphs and said, "You were really good with my geography assignment too."

The Cards bowed before her, and in unison, they uttered, "Our pleasure, Master."

As they arranged themselves into a neat pile in her hands, Sakura pondered, "I should thank Lee for teaching me Soul Resonance." An afterthought occurred to her, and it made her smile for some reason she couldn't quite figure out.

I mean, Xiaolang, she thought.

"By the way, Sakura," said Kero as he manoeuvred his player around a heavily armed centaur. "Now that ya got school back, ya still gonna do ya stuff 'round the neighbourhood?"

Sakura smiled, "On my way to school, I suppose."

* * *

The next day, Sakura rose bright and early. Kero, in his plush toy form, was still out like a light on his bed in Sakura's desk drawer. She checked to see that the game controllers had been nicely stowed away, and was glad that she wouldn't have to ban him from video games again. She hopped off her bed, changed into her school uniform, grabbed her bag, and was out the door.

While this was an early morning for Sakura, it was just a normal day for her elder brother, Touya. Her early morning rise didn't stop him from snickering, "Quit stompin' around, Kaiju."

Sakura turned and puffed out her cheeks.

"I'm not a Kaiju," she growled, her fist comically ready for the knockdown blow. Her threat didn't wipe the sadistic grin off Touya's face.

"Ooh, the MUTO stands no chance!" said Touya, as she walked toward the kitchen. Sakura's blood pressure spiked.

Her stress was gone in an instant the moment she saw the scrambled eggs and bacon set out for her on the table. Her father, Franklin, glanced over and gave her a warm smile.

"Morning, Dad," she said in English. Then she turned to the picture on the table and, in Japanese, said, "Good morning, Mum."

"You're up early," said Franklin.

"I've got morning duties, and the first day of term," said Sakura as she hoed into her breakfast.

"Oh no, the Kaiju is feasting!" exclaimed Touya. Sakura almost snapped her cutlery.

"Touya," said Franklin sternly. Smirking, he wagged a finger at the elder boy.

Touya just nodded, feigning remorse, and backed a bit down the hallway and out of Franklin's sight. Then, he mimed, "Kaiju!" which earned him a look from his sister that roared, "They'll never find your body!" But that just made Touya taunt her even more.

Franklin just laughed.

Sakura finished her breakfast and raced out the door. True, she did need to get to school early, but that wasn't the only reason for her speed. She forewent her rollerblades in favour of some running shoes, and darted down the street. When she was confident she was out of sight of her brother and father, she withdrew a bird-shaped key from under her shirt. She held it close and mumbled an incantation:

> *Key who conceals the Magic of Shadow,*
> *Ye who is more than ye seems:*
> *I command thee to bestow*
> *The power ye deems.*
> *Let us fulfil our vow*
> *In time's great streams … Release!*

The key shuddered in mid-air, and then grew into a long, pink, bird-head staff. She grabbed it, and then summoned a Card from the book in her backpack. It read 'Illusion.' Her eyes shone with green luminescence as she struck the Card with the beak of her staff. It received her mental command. In an instant, she was invisible to anyone who looked at her.

Perfect cover, she thought. *But before I start, I must have music!*

She donned her Bluetooth earphones and switched on her iPod. The sound of Kana Hanazawa's voice streamed into her ears with the song 'Ren'ai Circulation.' It instantly took hold of her body, and she danced her way down the road. Dissatisfied with the empty cherry blossom trees lining the path, she struck another Card, labelled 'Flower.'

The stagnant trees exploded with soft pink petals that propagated down the street like a wave.

Sakura trotted down the street to the beat of her music. She noticed a few kids burst onto the road, mesmerised by the sudden bloom of flowers. She saw a car careening toward them from an adjacent street. She struck a Card named 'Windy,' and a gust of air picked up the kids. The car passed harmlessly under them. Then, Sakura used a Card named 'Wood,' and a few branches from the trees nearby picked the kids up and put them safely on the side of the street. The amazed kids shrieked with delight, and danced under the branches, while Sakura sauntered right by them, unseen.

Sakura reached the edge of the street. She was nearing one of the busier parts of the Tokyo suburbs, and the street was pretty packed with cars. A bunch of early-morning commuters had piled up at the crossing. She turned her nose up at that, and summoned a Card with the name 'Jump.' The people around her felt a strange wind gust, but could not see the invisible girl with green glowing eyes, who soared over the traffic. She landed gracefully on the other side of the street.

She kept on moving through the town, toward her school. On the way, she saw an elderly lady struggling with her garden hose. She struck the Watery Card, and a tiny flash flood gently irrigated the woman's flowerbeds.

She heard a little boy nearby complain to his mother that the batteries in his game were dead, and sent the Thunder Card to pay those power cells a visit.

Passing by a park, she noticed a group of big middle-school boys picking on a smaller kid. She sent out the Shield Card to block the lead bully's fist, and then sent out Sword, Shadow, and Mirror. The bullies' bums suddenly became very acquainted with a flurry of sharp objects. As they rubbed their sore backsides, the bullies looked up and saw an army of their victim, as if he'd been cloned a dozen times. They panicked and scrambled away in fear, leaving alone a very confused but happy boy.

Though Sakura realised it was quite literally a superhero cliché, she saw a little girl crying that her cat was stuck in a tree. She summoned the Fly Card, which attached a set of wings to the befuddled feline and carried her into the girl's waiting arms.

At the next street, Sakura saw a baseball field. A lone gardener thereon cursed his lawnmower.

Have no fear, she thought as she held up a Card presenting a flame-clothed djinni, and the placard 'Fiery.' She struck it, and a bolt of red energy darted across the field and into the lawnmower's engine. It roared to life, and put a smile on the gardener's face.

On the same field, she saw a team of drillers with a light pole ready to erect, and a broken earth drill. Their dismayed frowns turned upside down when Sakura summoned the Earth Card, and whisked up a nice hole right where they wanted.

On the street where her school stood, Sakura passed by a bus stop. There sat a man alone. His dishevelled suit, five o'clock shadow, and depressed look told her he was a salary man, likely out of work. Her brow softened with sympathy, and she hit two Cards: Light and Dark. Beams of bright and dark energy encircled the man before diving into his temples. He shot up, a delighted, determined look on his face, and he marched down the street.

Sakura grinned and strutted toward her school, using her bird-head staff as a microphone to sing along with her music. She deactivated the wand and hung the key over her neck as she entered the school. But she could not stop dancing all the way to her classroom. She did the cha-cha all the way to her desk, a wide smile on her face. Her song finished, and she looked around the classroom.

There, in front of the blackboard, stood a Chinese boy no older than her. He was trying very hard not to laugh.

"Good morning, Xiaolang," stammered Sakura, her ears redder than a hot stove. "How much of that did you see?"

"About from when you disrupted the cherry blossom blooming cycle," returned Xiaolang, his merriment cracking his voice a few times.

Sakura fumed with embarrassment. She pushed past her frustration and exclaimed, "And what're you doing here? You're not in my class."

Xiaolang shrugged, "I wanted to say 'hi.' Hope you had a good summer holiday."

"I did," said Sakura. Her embarrassment started to subside and her cheerful nature reasserted itself. "I've been using the Cards to make people happy all over. Kero thought it was an awesome idea, since I'd be kinda like a superhero."

Xiaolang pursed his lips and said, "Just be careful, you hear? You don't want to be outed as a magic girl. Plus, it's not a good idea to meddle too much in the lives of others. Lots of very smart people have done the same thing with this kind of power, and it hasn't ended well."

Sakura slumped. Her mind cooked up a dozen scenarios where her magic would go wrong, and each of them made her question her decisions. Sensing her unease, Xiaolang walked over and rested his hand on her shoulder.

"Don't worry, Kinomoto," he said. "You're an excellent Clow Master. I can't imagine what it would have been like if Alice Axolotl had gotten those Cards."

Sakura beamed. The mention of that rogue Cardcaptor Witch reminded her of the night she had captured the last of the Cards. It had been then that she proved herself to Yue, Kero's lunar counterpart.

"Speaking of which," she began. "Did you figure out where that fake Sealing Staff came from?"

"I sent it to my family in Hong Kong so they can analyse it," said Xiaolang.

"You aren't going back yet?" asked Sakura. The thought depressed her a little.

"Not yet," said Xiaolang. "My parents told me to stay

for the rest of the year, since it's already been paid for. I'm actually glad. Poker night with my classmates is fun." He added with a shudder, "But also, I'd rather not be around that serpent staff. Just thinking about it still makes my skin crawl. Mother and Father haven't been able to identify its maker yet."

"What about that place you mentioned? W-M-A-D?" asked Sakura.

"Oh, DWMA? Yeah, they don't like me or my family," replied Xiaolang with a wave of his hand. "Philosophical differences, you see?"

Sakura cocked her head, completely oblivious to his meaning. She wanted to ask more, but was certain it would be complicated. Plus, she needed to finish her morning duties.

"Let's meet up for lunch," she said as Xiaolang headed for the door.

"That'd be nice, Kinomoto," he said over his shoulders.

"Xiaolang!" she called after him. He stopped and turned. She smiled and said, "Call me 'Sakura.'"

That made Xiaolang blush, and he bolted out of the room.

Sakura sighed with contentment, though she wasn't sure from where it came. But that didn't matter. As she set to work cleaning the desks and writing the date on the board, she thought to herself, *This will be a good semester!*

2 | A New Teacher

Sakura finished writing the date on the board, just as a magical clone of her dusted off the last desk. A small gust of wind had rounded all the dirt on the floor into a neat pile, while a shadowy hand swept it into a dustpan. The trees outside had seemingly grown hands out of their branches, with which they were batting clear the chalkboard erasers.

Sakura turned to find the room spick and span.

"Well done, everyone!" she exclaimed. She picked up the bird-head staff on the desk nearby, and waved it in the air like a conductor's baton. The trees tossed the erasers into the classroom, and a soft wind carried them to the chalkboard sill. Then bolts of black, green, and cyan light whisked through the air toward Sakura's school bag, taking their rightful forms as Clow Cards in the front pocket. However, Sakura's doppelganger remained.

"Umm … Master?" asked Mirror meekly.

Man, it's so weird hearing my own voice like that, thought Sakura.

"What is it, Mirror?" she asked. Her doppelganger started to stammer and shuffle. She was clearly struggling to find the right words, and Sakura took pity on her. She put her hand on Mirror's shoulder and said, "Should we resonate?"

Though soft and well-spoken, the voice of a girl ripped

through the classroom like a blaring klaxon. A wave of horror ripped through Sakura, who feareds that her magic powers had been discovered. She turned in fright, and then sighed with relief at the sight of her best friend.

"Tomoyo, don't scare me like that," she exclaimed.

Tomoyo just smiled, belying her prankish inner nature. She waltzed past the pair of identical twins and popped down at her usual desk. She eyed Mirror and said, "You'd best skedaddle, before someone else shows up."

Sakura turned to Mirror with a sigh. "She's right. How about we talk later?"

Mirror looked saddened, and she gazed down at her toes. After a brief build up, she finally grabbed Sakura's hands and said, "The others asked me to tell you, we really like you as our Master. And we're with you one hundred per cent!"

Bewildered, Sakura smiled and nodded delightedly. Satisfied, Mirror dematerialised into a Card and wafted into her Master's schoolbag.

Sakura fell at her desk with a huff.

"It may look easy, but magic really is hard," she said. Tomoyo gave no response, so Sakura looked over at her friend. At first, she thought Tomoyo was surfing on her phone. Then she saw the screen, displaying a video of Mirror making her pledge of support. Tomoyo's eyes glimmered with excitement, while Sakura's face reacquainted itself with her palms.

"But it was such a powerful moment," Tomoyo insisted. "This is going right up on my Cardcaptor Sakura website."

"Tomoyo!" complained Sakura. "Sooner or later, people will suspect things."

"Pah! All they'll learn is the supreme greatness and all-round world-destroying cuteness that is my beloved Sakura!" exclaimed Tomoyo.

Sakura gave a dismayed chuckle.

Not long after Tomoyo's appearance did students start

flooding into the school. Before long, the classroom was full of students, eager to start the new semester. First, Naoko turned up and started raving about how she finally finished reading *The Wheel Of Time*. Unfortunately, she stayed up so late over the summer break that she didn't really relax much.

"But it was so worth it," she said with a yawn.

Then, in came Takeshi. The boy strode up to the group and proclaimed, "Good morning, all. Glad to finally be starting the new semester." Before anyone could respond, Takeshi immediately raised his finger excitedly. "Did you know about *semesters*? The kanji, when you say it, sounds like *school tree*. That's because, before Reginald Von Datesmith invented the calendar, school semesters went from when a tree in the middle of the school started growing a new branch. The semester continued until the branch was longer than the shortest child was tall."

"Oh, dear," said Tomoyo.

If only they still measured semesters like that, pondered Sakura, as she thought of the Wood Card in her school bag.

"But that would take such a long time, especially if the shortest child was really tall," said Naoko.

"Yes, indeed," said Takeshi, getting right in Naoko's face. "They say that they always enrolled at least one toddler, so the term wouldn't be too long. However, the toddler always caused a ruckus because —" Takeshi was suddenly jerked back by the collar.

Chiharu grabbed him by the scruff of the neck and growled, "Could you be less of a fibber? Seriously! All summer I had to put up with you!"

Takeshi chortled as Chiharu shook him furiously. All Tomoyo, Naoko, and Sakura could do was laugh at it. Soon after, the bell rang, and in walked the homeroom teacher. Ever the diligent representative, Naoko led the class to stand, bow, and sit. The homeroom teacher gave his typical new semester speech, loaded with encouragement and enthusiasm for the next few months of school.

Then he made a special announcement.

"It is my honour to introduce a new student teacher," he said. "He's from Scotland, and he is studying education. He will be serving this semester as an assistant English teacher."

He called out to the hall and invited the individual to enter. A boy, barely older than Touya, strode in. Despite his clean-shaven spotless face, crowned by red-tinged hair, and a gleaming glance that would put a supermodel to shame, the boy was clearly very nervous. He rigidly marched toward the front of the class and gauchely cleared his throat.

"I am Eriol Lamperouge," he stammered in well-practiced Japanese.

Of course, Sakura could pick out the Scottish tinge to his vowels, and it made her smile with endearment. And, despite not being able to see her friend's face, Tomoyo could just sense Sakura's expression and she giggled.

*I just **love** knowing everything,* she thought.

Eriol looked as if he was about to cry when the homeroom teacher asked if any of the students had questions. They had quite a lot. Some of them were related to where in Scotland he was from. Others involved why he had a French-sounding surname. Naoko really hit on the money, when she asked why he had the same name as a character from J. R. R. Tolkien. To be fair, Eriol's Japanese was enough to answer most, but he was clearly very flustered by the end of it all. His face was red and his hairline a little damp. The teacher must have taken pity and asked him to sit by the side.

Sakura kept any questions she had to herself, not wishing to bother the boy further. Plus, she could sate her curiosity on his terms – unlike her non-English-speaking friends.

Homeroom finished, and classes progressed at a slow

pace. It was annoying enough for Sakura, who really wanted to converse with Eriol. She couldn't figure out why, but didn't really care. There was just something about him that drew her interest. In between classes, Tomoyo couldn't help but tease, "I think Tsukishiro has another love-rival?"

"No, don't be silly, Tomoyo," retorted Sakura. "He's just interesting. And sure, we all speak English at home on Sundays. But it'll just be nice to talk to someone else in English ... you know, other than my brother and Dad."

Tomoyo chortled, "Oh, well, you know, Lee speaks English, doesn't he?"

Sakura pursed her lips and shot evils at her friend. It only made Tomoyo giggle even more.

Finally, classes finished and it was time for lunch. Sakura quickly finished her lunchbox and then left the classroom. She strode out into the school courtyard, where she saw Eriol hunched over a dictionary while nibbling at a sandwich. She almost reconsidered bothering him, but decided to push her luck and tapped him on the shoulder. The poor boy jumped almost three feet in the air and choked on his food.

He stammered furiously, "Ah, umm ... nice to meet you, Miss ..."

"It's Kinomoto," said Sakura, still in Japanese. "I was in the class you were introduced to this morning. Class 2-C?"

"Oh, yes, I remember," said Eriol, offering his hand to shake. He immediately snatched it back. "Oh, umm, Sorry."

"Why is that, Mister Lamperouge?" asked Sakura, quite befuddled.

"Oh," the boy paused, his brow knitted in hard concentration. "It's just ... I once was introduced to a Muslim woman, and I tried to shake her hand. Let's just say, in Islamic culture, that's more disrespectful than looking up her dress. Since then, I've been a little jittery about trying to shake any girl's hand."

"Well, *I've* got no problem," said Sakura politely. She offered her hand, and the boy shook it nervously.

He released it and let out a sigh. "So, what can I do for you, Miss Kinomoto?"

"I just wanted to say 'hello' and learn a little bit about you, if that's alright," said Sakura, taking a seat next to him.

Eriol groaned, "I suppose that's fine. But my Japanese still takes a lot of thought. I'm not really confident."

Sakura's smile widened and she said, "Perhaps I could speak in English?"

Her accent caught Eriol right off-guard, and he exclaimed, "You're British!?" His Scottish accent came right through, making Sakura giggle.

"On my Dad's side," she said. "Lived in Surrey for a few years. Did kindergarten through to second grade there."

Eriol looked like he'd just been given a lifeline, and he clutched his chest with relief. He relaxed noticeably and said, "Well, what did you want to know?"

"What made you want to come to Japan?" asked Sakura.

"Well, I'd made a promise to my father," said Eriol. "Our family was already well-off, but he wanted me to expand my horizons and learn as much as I could about the world. So, here I am."

Sakura looked him up and down and said, "You look a little young."

"I'm about eighteen," said Eriol. "I was accelerated through gifted programs."

Sakura whistled and asked, "And you came from Scotland, right?"

"Aye, grew up in Aberdeen," said Eriol laxly. "But I moved to a place in Glastonbury,s when my mother and father passed."

Sakura choked, recalling a similar incident with her beloved Yukito at the Aquarium. With a cringe, she said,

"I'm sorry to hear that."

"Ah, never mind," said Eriol. "Happened a long while back, and I've had people to look after me." He quickly waved off the subject and asked, "So, you lived in Britain a while?"

"Uh-huh," replied Sakura. "My Dad was a British archaeologist, and my Mum a Japanese model. We lived in Britain so that my elder brother and I could learn English. But then, my Mum got sick, and we decided to move back to Japan."

Eriol's face softened. "Did your mother recover?"

"Unfortunately, no," said Sakura solemnly. "But the doctors were really good and she was comfortable for years longer than they thought. And I'm not lonely. I've got my Dad and Big Brother ... even if he's a bit of a bully."

That made Eriol chuckle, "Big Brothers, eh?"

Sakura recalled all the vexing moments she had with Touya and pouted almost comically. "That meanie keeps calling me 'Kaiju' ... Oh, that means 'strange beast.'"

Eriol's jaw dropped with bewilderment. "How terrible!"

"He's nice sometimes," replied Sakura. "But my Dad is *always* nice! Except when I don't do my homework on time. He grounds me until I get it all done."

"Then he's doing the right thing by you," said Eriol, his finger pointed fixedly at her. "He's a good Dad, it sounds like." Sakura nodded, smiling at the image of her father. Eriol went on, "So, I assume you have friends?"

"Oh, yes," exclaimed Sakura. "I have my friends Tomoyo, Xiaolang, and Kero too!"

Eriol frowned. "K-Kero? What? As in, a frog?"

Oh, nuts, I let my mouth slip, thought Sakura in a panic. She went into a fit of stammers and gasps as Eriol rubbed his jaw.

"Where have I heard that before?" he wondered. He looked at her, and a realisation struck him. "You're that

Cardcaptor girl from YouTube! Kero's your sidekick!"

Sakura hugged herself in order to contain her embarrassment.

"You watch Tomoyo's show too, don't you?" she mumbled.

"Only a few episodes," said Eriol. "But I see little girls all over Dublin dressing up like you. Girls all over love you! I suppose you get requests all the time to be a movie star or something."

Sakura gripped her cheeks and squealed, "Anything but that! It's so embarrassing!"

Eriol just grinned and shook his head in amazement. His gaze went up to the sky and he mumbled, "I should thank my lucky stars I landed in a school with an English-speaking celebrity. It'll be nice that I can relax my brain once in a while."

"Oh, if you want, I can introduce you to Xiaolang Lee," said Sakura, her embarrassment subsiding. "He's from Hong Kong, and he speaks really good English too."

"Xiaolang?" intoned Eriol. "Don't Japanese people use each other's surnames?"

Sakura shrugged. "He called me 'Sakura' once, and I decided it was okay so long as I could call him 'Xiaolang.'"

Eriol's eyes shifted and he asked, "Then, is it alright for me to call you 'Sakura' too?"

Sakura's eyebrows went up and she said, "That seems okay, so long as I can call you 'Eriol.'"

Eriol grinned and held out his hand. "Well then, Sakura. I look forward to being your teacher."

Sakura shook it and said, "I look forward to being your student, Eriol."

* * *

Sakura was oblivious to the two pairs of eyes nestled into the bushes nearby, watching her little chat with the new substitute teacher. One of those pairs was watching it through the camera app on her phone.

"It's almost like the first meeting scene in a romance novel," chortled Tomoyo.

The other spy gripped the branch of the tree tightly. Tomoyo could almost hear the hard wood squishing beneath Xiaolang's tightening grip. She glanced over at him, and saw a truly enraged glare. The boy's confession at the Tsukimine Shrine a few weeks back came to mind, and she understood his jealousy straight away.

That only intensified her salacious hunger for chaos.

Oh ho ho ho, this'll be so much fun, she thought.

Not even the gathering rain-clouds overhead could dampen her spirits.

3 | The Deluge

When Sakura reached her house, the sky was a thick blanket of dark clouds. A healthy rumbling echoed from above, forewarning an imminent downpour. She was glad she'd foregone gymnastics practice in exchange for an early afternoon arrival. She didn't have an umbrella, and just knew she would've been drenched.

Much to her non-surprise, Kero was still in her room, pounding away at her video games. He hardly noticed her enter the bedroom, until she accidentally discarded her shirt on his tiny head.

"No! My game!" cried the living teddy bear. He scrambled out from under the shirt and saw his health bar reach zero, accompanied by the insufferable title of 'Game Over.' He floated into the air and tossed the school shirt back at his Master. "You messed up my game!" he cried.

Sakura pursed her lips and said, "Nice to see you too, Kero. Did you have a good day?" Kero panted, rubbed his head, and yawned. "Judging from your bloodshot eyes, you've spent the whole day on that thing."

"I was about to beat the big boss too," snapped Kero.

"I'm sure you saved your game before going up against him," said Sakura with a shrug. She walked over to the desk and started on her homework.

Kero didn't let up. "I was so close to beating him! And

now you broke my state of Zen!"

"State of Zen?" asked Sakura with a raised eyebrow.

"I was in the zone, girl," moaned Kero. He started to falter in mid-air as his eyelids dragged themselves shut. He fell onto Sakura's desk and gripped his head. "Now, I ain't holdin' up over my sleepiness. Gah! My eyes're killin' me! And my head!"

Sakura gazed at her homework and let out a long sigh. She picked him up onto her shoulder and said, "That's because you're fatigued, dehydrated, and hungry. I'll get you some food."

She went down to the kitchen, made him a few sandwiches and a long drink of water to wash them down, and then walked back up to her room. The Beast of the Seal curled up on Sakura's bed, leaving his Master alone to focus on her homework. She quickly finished the math and Japanese drills, and was part way through her prescribed reading when she heard the front door open. She capped her highlighter, packed everything away, and walked downstairs.

There was Franklin at the front door, the top of his head and his shoulders absolutely soaked. He shook off his umbrella and gave a bewildered sigh. He saw his daughter greet him and he exclaimed, "Where did all this rain come from?"

Only then did Sakura notice the torrential downpour. The roadside catchments managed to drain the water faster than it came, keeping the footpath from flooding. Unfortunately, the roof gutters were overflowing. All Sakura could do was raise her eyebrows in amazement.

"The weather had forecasted rain," said Franklin. "But I wasn't expecting this."

"Hopefully, it won't get worse," said Sakura.

Franklin closed the door and regarded her with a smile. "I'll need a bath, and then I'll get started on dinner. How does spaghetti sound?"

"Great! Would you like me to start it?" asked Sakura.

"That way, we won't eat too late."

Franklin smirked. "Do I take that long?"

Sakura grinned. "I've always wondered how many times you shampoo your hair."

Franklin chortled with jesting indignation before strutting up the stairs. Meanwhile, Sakura trotted off to the kitchen and started chopping onions and garlic. She wiped away the last of her onion tears as her father walked in, his hair still slightly damp. He took over cooking while hearing Sakura talk about her day. He was especially interested in the Scottish teacher.

"And he's only eighteen?" he asked.

"He said he got to skip grades," said Sakura.

Franklin turned to her and said, "Make sure he doesn't get too close."

Sakura cringed. "Oh, Dad, it's not like that."

"I know, and I'm sure he's good," said Franklin. "But I just want to say it, otherwise I'll fret. You're seventeen this year, but *he's* a teacher. He needs to be respectful."

Sakura smiled as she recalled Eriol's initial refusal to shake her hand.

"He is," she said.

Since Touya was (as Sakura would put it) at one of his gazzilion part-time jobs, it was just the two of them – a Daddy-Daughter Night, as Franklin sometimes called it. They continued their chitchat long after the meal was finished, discussing Tomoyo's ongoing plans for future Cardcaptor videos, and Franklin's recent considerations to get back into research.

"What kind of research?" asked Sakura as she wiped the colander dry.

"Well, it looks like there's a new excavation site near Odai Yamamoto," Franklin explained. "A few new artefacts have been found from Ancient Japan, from about sixteen thousand years ago." Sakura's eyes bugged out. Franklin chuckled, "I know! Those artefacts might be interesting to study."

Sakura's smile widened and she said, "I'm glad you're taking an interest. Hope it works out well for you."

Franklin returned the smile and gave his daughter a big hug. Then, he decided to get an early night. Sakura finished drying the dishes. Then, she put a small amount of leftover spaghetti in a bowl, and took it up to Kero. He ate his dinner while Sakura finished her prescribed reading. Then, they played a little bit of *Super Mario Odyssey* in cooperative mode.

Outside, it still rained heavily. At the very least, there was no thunder. The pitter-patter of fat water drops on their roof was quite a soothing sound, and it made both of them quite drowsy. After a quick bath, Sakura snuggled up in her bed, and Kero retreated to his little desk-drawer apartment.

It was a quiet, uneventful night, to which both had grown accustomed. They were content. So content, in fact, that they didn't wake when the Shadow Key laying on Sakura's desk started to glow.

* * *

It read eight in the morning on Sakura's clock, but she wouldn't have known it from the gloom trickling through her window. When she saw the time, she freaked, and scrambled to get changed. Kero woke up not long after and yawned.

"Jeez, Sakura," he moaned. "You need to buy a few more alarm clocks."

"I forgot to set this one," cried Sakura. As she yanked on her school uniform, Kero floated out of his drawer and gazed out the window. He could barely see the house next door through the downpour. He frowned, his ears twitching and flexing.

Sakura didn't notice his fixation and raced out of the room. When she reached the kitchen, she found Touya and Franklin eating breakfast.

"Oh no, the Kaiju's attacking!" exclaimed Touya.

Sakura raised a clenched fist and growled, "Say that again?"

"Okay, now, don't start a ruckus," said Franklin. Noting Sakura's uniform, he added, "Don't worry about being late. I got a call saying school has been cancelled on account of the rain."

While Sakura was relieved to not be tardy for school, she was a little disappointed. She ate breakfast at a much more relaxed rate with her father and brother. Then she went up stairs, changed, and called Tomoyo.

"Yes, I'm at home too," said Tomoyo. "Apparently, there was a flooding at the school."

"I hope no one got hurt," said Sakura as she stretched out on her bed. She considered going back to sleep. "It's a shame though, I was hoping to see you and Xiaolang again."

"What about Mister Lamperouge?" asked Tomoyo sneakily.

"Tomoyo!" cried Sakura. "He's a teacher. And plus, my heart still goes to Yukito."

"Even though he's Yue?" asked Tomoyo.

"That just makes it even better," said Sakura. "He can come out with me on our adventures."

Tomoyo gave a long sigh. "Unfortunately, we haven't had much in the way of adventures since Yue. Why don't we make a movie instead?"

"A movie?" repeated Sakura.

"Yes! I've already been getting requests on our channel for a movie, and I'm sure there's a lot of people who would back us for it. So why not make a movie? Ah! My dear Sakura would be a bigger star than Jennifer Lawrence!"

Sakura could only groan, knowing that Tomoyo had started upon her ghastly hair-brained schemes yet again. And poor Sakura was only along for the ride. She cringed in anticipation that Kero would soon swoop in and start plotting with Tomoyo about all the ways to make him look cool.

That didn't happen.

It was then that Sakura looked around the room for her friend. He hadn't moved from the windowsill. His dish-shaped ears continued to twitch like a radar array. Sakura saw his fixed gaze, and knew the wheels in his head were revving.

"Tomoyo, I'll call you back," she said, and promptly hung up the phone. She approached Kero and asked, "Are you sensing anything?"

"I keep gettin' a whiff of somethin'," he whispered. He winced and growled, "I keep missin' it. I can't figure it out. There's somethin' 'bout this rain."

"It's not another Clow Card, is it?" asked Sakura.

"No, you got all the Cards," said Kero. "Maybe if me and the Cards resonate, I can figure out what it is." He floated over to the desk-drawer and pulled it open with his mind. His eyes bugged out at the sight of what was supposed to have been the Book of Clow.

"Kero, look at this," said Sakura, holding up what she thought was the Shadow Key. Instead of a bird's head at the end of the key, there was a star-shaped topaz set into a ring of pink metal. Tiny wings adorned either side of it.

"You think that's weird?" he said. "Take a look at this?" He levitated the book in her drawer. It was indeed as ornate and beautifully crafted as the Book of Clow, but its colour was pink beneath the gold and silver filigree. A large jewel, cut in the shape of a star, was emblazoned into the front cover, above which sat a placard with the name 'Sakura.'

"What's going on here?" she exclaimed. "What is this now, the Book of Sakura?"

Kero shrugged in amazement. He willed it open and found the Clow Cards inside. When Sakura held them in her hands, they felt cold. She reached out through the resonance link to speak to them. But they didn't respond. It was as if they weren't even there.

Panic filled Sakura and she exclaimed, "Kero! What happened to the Cards?"

Kero looked her dead in the eyes, his own radiating panic and concern.

"Get Snow-Rabbit and the Brat," he barked. "Have 'em meet us at Tomoyo's place."

* * *

Though the downpour was a nightmare, Tomoyo's chauffeur managed the roads with skill. Sakura really had to give him credit for that. And even though there were a few dangerous spots, the man kept his cool all the way through it, even if Sakura didn't. She was glad when they finally made it to the Daidouji mansion, and pulled into one of its many undercover car parks.

The mansion's staff stood at the ready with towels and cups of tea for the guests Tomoyo expected. As usual, Tomoyo's mother, Sonomi, went ballistic over Sakura, and showered her with excited hugs. They went to Tomoyo's room, which was just as big as Sakura remembered it. Yukito and Xiaolang were already present.

As soon as Sakura saw Yukito, she almost forgot why she was there, and she beamed excitedly.

"Thanks for coming, Yukito!" she exclaimed.

"Of course, Sakura," said Yukito with that dashing smile she adored so. "I must admit, I'm excited to be here. Here's where Cardcaptor Sakura comes to life, isn't it?"

"Yep," said Tomoyo proudly.

"If you four need anything, please let me know," said Sonomi as she closed the door.

At that moment, Kero soared out of Sakura's bag and gasped, "Gah! Thought I was gonna die in that car!" He eyed Xiaolang and sneered, "What up, Brat?"

"Local precipitation, for one, Fluffy," retorted Xiaolang.

Kero eyed Yukito. The boy only smiled back at him. The reflex to play dead around him was still very much present, but Kero managed to supress it. He just said, "Yue can hear us fine?"

Yukito nodded with a smile that made Kero's skin crawl.

"I won't transform though," he said. "We both think it's best for Sakura's secrecy."

Yue smilin' like that is just creepy, thought the Beast of the Seal.

"So, why have you brought us here?" asked Xiaolang.

"Did you want to pitch them my movie idea?" asked Tomoyo, her eyes gleaming.

"No, sorry," said Sakura. She took the book and key out of her bag and showed it to them. "Those used to be the Book of Clow and the Shadow Key. They changed last night." She opened the book and showed them the Clow Cards. As soon as Yukito and Xiaolang touched them, they inhaled sharply.

Yukito looked horrified. "It's as if —"

"They're dead," said Xiaolang with a deadpanned tone.

Sakura shrieked as tears raced toward her eyes. Tomoyo grabbed her and held her trembling body tightly.

"Hang on," said Kero, pre-empting her mourning. He kept his eyes on his Master and waited for her to calm down. Then he gazed at Yukito and said, "Resonate with me."

Yukito sat up straight, and held his hands palm-up on his knees. Kero assumed a similar posture, and they both started to glow. The faintest light wafted from the Cards on the table. They sat like that for at least a minute, before their glow subsided and they relaxed.

"The Cards ain't dead," said Kero. He gave Sakura the thumbs-up. "Don't worry. They can't die. They're just dormant."

Sakura wrung her hands nervously. "Then, what do I do to make them not dormant?"

"I dunno," said Kero.

"Maybe she needs to use them," said Xiaolang. "They

might've just gone to sleep."

Sakura exchanged glances with Kero, who nodded. Then, she took the key and held it up.

> *Key who conceals the Magic of Shadow,*
> *Ye who is more than ye seems:*
> *I command thee to bestow*
> *The power ye deems.*
> *Let us fulfil our vow*
> *In time's great streams ... Release!*

Nothing happened.

She repeated the incantation, but the key just sat there, quiet and inert.

* * *

The drive back home through the rain was just as arduous as before. The rain and wind pounded the car, but Sakura could hardly be bothered. She just sat there. She slipped a hand into her pocket and gripped the deck of inert Clow Cards, as she would the hand of a dying friend. She felt utterly miserable.

Xiaolang's words echoed in her head: *I'll consult my parents in Hong Kong. They have Clow's extensive library, so they're sure to know something.*

It did little to assuage Sakura's fears.

Kero peeked out of her bag and exchanged glances with Yukito, who felt equally helpless. Eventually, Yukito reached over and gripped Sakura's hand. The gesture electrified Sakura's arm, as did his words.

"Don't worry, Sakura," said the boy. "Remember your invincible spell?"

Sakura's heart swelled a little, and she recited, "I'll definitely be alright." She smiled weakly, but in her mind she still felt powerless.

"Uh-oh," mumbled Yukito. Sakura and Kero snapped to attention, and realised their car was floating.

Sakura leaned forward. "Mister driver? What's going on?"

"I believe we're floating, Ma'am," said the driver, a little panicked.

The car started to drift faster. Sakura and Yukito checked out the windows. The road was flooding. Sakura shrieked at the cold water that licked at her ankles. Yukito quickly unlocked the door and pushed as hard as he could against the rising water. But he didn't share his alter ego's strength. Even when Sakura helped, the door wouldn't budge.

Suddenly, a tremendous gust of wind struck the car and sent it tumbling. The occupants shrieked and cried in horror as they fell head-over-heels in the confined box. Out the corner of her eye, Sakura saw the Arakawa River, into which the car crashed unceremoniously.

Water now rushed into the confined car, and evicting precious air. Sakura pulled her face out of the water. She was dizzy and could hardly recognise the red patch where her head had been. Blood seeped from a small gash in her forehead. She looked around in a panic and saw Yukito tending to the driver.

The boy looked at Kero, floating face up in the water, and barked, "Driver's unconscious! Let's go!"

They both flashed white. Kero became his winged lion form, and Yukito's jeans and shirt morphed into an ornate changsham robe. Yue grabbed the driver and deployed his wings. Kero unleashed a fireball from his mouth to blow the roof off the car. The two magical beings pulled Sakura and the driver out of the wreck and flew toward the riverbank.

The rain buffeted them from all sides. Sakura could hardly find air to breathe amid the torrent. She couldn't open her eyes to see where Kero was taking her as the water just kept striking her, harder and harder.

She heard Yue's strident voice bellow over the wind, but couldn't make out the words. Of course, she could hear the fear in his voice. A second later, a wall of water smacked her out of Kero's grip. She tumbled through the water currents that seemed determined to drown her, until her hands found a sturdy pole by the riverbank, and she held onto it for dear life. The water subsided enough for her to reach the surface, and she gasped for air.

She opened her eyes a crack and saw two pillars of water. Kero and Yue floated within them, tendrils of fluid binding their limbs and strangling them.

This has to be another Clow Card, she thought. Yet she couldn't sense anything, even when extending her perception as far as it would go. Desperately, she pulled out the key and recited the incantation.

Still, nothing happened.

"Come on! Release!" she screamed. But nothing happened.

Why have my powers gone? I gathered the Clow Cards and became their Master. I proved myself to Xiaolang, and to Yue. And now, Kero and Yue are going to drown because I failed.

The image of her mother crept into her confused mind. She stood in a field of stars.

Stars ... Like the key ...

The words echoed in her mind.

New key, new wand ... New incantation.

A series of words and phrases surged through her mind, as if guided by a being from another world. She held out the key, swinging in the wind and rain, and began to chant:

> *Key of the Stars, Master of dreams,*
> *Bequeath unto me the power ye deems.*
> *Let us fulfil our vow in time's great streams ... Release!*

The key glimmered with light brighter than the sun. It blasted away the rain as it grew into a new wand. The star-shaped gem at its end shone with internal light that stood out as a lighthouse in the storm.

Sakura sighed with delight. She reached into her pocket and procured the Watery Card. Yet, even when she touched it to her new wand, it did nothing.

"New wand," she intoned. "So, new Cards!"

She reached out to the Card with her mind and sought out the dormant magical power within it. Another incantation flowed through her mind, and she uttered it without a second thought:

> *Card of Clow, thy magic innate,*
> *Discard thy form and reincarnate.*
> *Ye serve, hence, under a new Master:*
> *Sakura of the Shining Star.*

The Card shimmered and flashed. A cloud of fine dust wafted off the Card as if it had shed its skin. What Sakura held was no longer Watery, but something of a new form. She threw it out in front of her and held up the Star Wand.

"Calm this storm, Aqua!" she roared.

The Card morphed into the majestic piscine humanoid she knew as Watery, and yet he was different. His scales radiated a new spectrum of white and green that danced through the rainy sky. He started to swirl about the pillars of water, before diving through them and blasting them apart. He caught Yue and Kero and delivered them to the bank of the river. Then he shot into the sky and parted the clouds.

The clouds gave one last grumble before the rain finally came to a stop. The Arakawa River withdrew into its usual stream, allowing Sakura a chance to set her feet down on the soggy ground. Her new Card flew out of the sky. The piscine creature approached her and bowed reverently.

"Many thanks for my new form, Master," said his voice in her mind. He then morphed back into a Card in Sakura's hand.

She gazed at it. The creature had assumed a new pose upon the Card, which glittered as Sakura tilted it. The placard below the picture read, 'Aqua,' just as she had named it.

Sakura smiled and pocketed the new Card. She saw Kero and Yue coming to their senses nearby. But, as she lifted her foot to step toward them, a tremendous fatigue overcame her and she blacked out.

4 | Concealment

Sakura sighed deeply as she opened her eyes. Her eyelids stung with the bite of sleep-dust, and she wiped it away with a yawn. As she stretched, she let out an involuntary groan, through which she could hear Tomoyo's voice, nervously calling for help.

She looked over, and saw her friend sitting at her bedside. Only, it wasn't her bed. She quickly noticed the periodic beep of monitors beside her, the itch of a bandage over her head, and the IV in her arm.

"What's going on?" she asked obliviously. "Why am I in the hospital?"

A doctor approached, with Franklin, Touya, and Yukito in tow. Touya's friend was in a hospital gown with a few bandages on his face. All her family had anxious looks, and wrung their hands nervously.

The doctor checked her vitals and flashed a penlight in her eyes. Then he stepped back and asked, "Do you know your name?"

"Umm ... Sakura Kinomoto," she said. She then turned to Franklin and asked, "Dad, what's going on?"

Franklin's worried expression cracked with a smile and he said, "You were in an accident on the way back from Daidouji's place."

Tomoyo looked as if she were on the verge of tears. Before she could unleash her worry, the doctor interjected.

"Just answer the questions, and then you can talk," said the doctor, his eyes locked on her. "You recognise everyone here?"

Sakura looked at Tomoyo and said her name, much to the black-haired girl's grieved delight. Then she looked at Yukito and said his name. She pointed out her father and said his name. Then she pointed at Touya. Her vindictive side took over and she said, "I don't know you at all!"

Touya's jaw tightened.

But Sakura couldn't keep a straight face and she burst into laughter before saying, "That's my silly Big Brother, Touya."

Touya scoffed and tightened his arms around his chest.

"Kaiju," he muttered.

Franklin and Yukito shuffled nervously, while Tomoyo trembled.

The doctor finally explained. "You were in a car accident last night. Evidently, the Arakawa River flooded and your car was swept away. Thankfully, your friend managed to pull you and your driver out of the car. You're also lucky that the rain let up when it did, otherwise the ambulance might not have reached you in time."

"We thought you might have had brain damage, since you wouldn't wake up," said Tomoyo. "But, everything's alright now, Doctor?"

"We'll keep you a while for observation, but everything seems fine," said the doctor. Satisfied, he left the room and the men released long sighs of relief. Tomoyo finally let her emotions out in a huge wave. She threw herself onto Sakura and cried into her shoulder.

"Tomoyo, it's alright," cooed Sakura.

"I should have been with you in the car," cried Tomoyo. "I should have offered you stay the night. You almost died!"

"I'm fine now," said Sakura as she stroked her friend's hair. "Yukito was there with me, so I was definitely alright."

Franklin turned to Yukito and threw his arms around him.

"Thank you so much for saving my daughter, Mister Tsukishiro," he said warmly.

Yukito beamed, "Of course, Mister Kinomoto. Sakura's like family to me."

Sakura looked over Tomoyo's shoulder and smiled at Yukito.

I should thank Yue as well, she thought.

For the moment, the whole room was filled with a loving atmosphere. But Franklin cut it short when he said, "I just need to go and speak to the doctor. I'll be back." And he left.

Not long after, Yukito excused himself for a toilet break. By then, Sakura and Tomoyo were chatting about various things, and Touya took the chance to slip out of the room and chase after his friend. He, of course, knew something was afoot. He'd smelled the wrongness in the rain last night, and was certain it had something to do with Sakura's other life.

He saw Yukito emerge from the toilet and jogged down the hall toward him.

"What's the matter?" asked Yukito.

"Yuki, I need to talk to you," said Touya. His voice became shaky and he started to stammer. "Look... umm... all this stuff about Sakura's videos. I hear you're getting into them too."

"Oh yeah, they asked me to play a character," said Yukito. "You're not jealous, are you?"

"No, nothing like that," groaned Touya. "It's just... I know that —"

"Mister Tsukishiro," interjected one of the nurses. "The doctor would like to run a pre-discharge check. If you'll come with me, please."

"Oh, of course," said Yukito. He smiled apologetically to Touya. "We'll chat later, okay?"

"Yeah," mumbled Touya. He chewed his tongue

irritably as he watched his friend scurry down the hall.

"You shouldn't bother him just yet," said a familiar female voice. Touya swivelled and saw the ghost of his mother, Nadeshiko. He almost blurted a retort, but noticed the people around him. He nodded to an empty patient room nearby, and Nadeshiko followed him as he shut the door behind them.

"Why shouldn't I, Mum?" asked Touya. "I know Yukito's not human, and I know something's happening with Sakura. I should just up and tell them, so then they can focus on the problem instead of cooking up crap about it."

"Trust me, Touya, all you'll do is trouble Yukito," said Nadeshiko.

Touya pursed his lips as his body trembled with worry. His mind wandered to the expression he'd seen on his friend's face when the ambulance brought them to the hospital. The boy had seemed terrified and worried, but also angry. Yukito had tried to conceal it from Touya, but he could see it all the same.

"He needs my powers," said Touya resolutely. "If I give them to him, he won't ..." His eyes started to water.

Nadeshiko placed a hand on his cheek and said, "Give Sakura time. She'll grow stronger. Just you watch."

Images of Sakura's morning behaviour ripped through Touya's mind. Visions of her poor attentiveness and clumsiness spurred a fire of panic and fear. He looked into his mother's eyes and saw that same firm look that he could not refuse.

"I'll wait," he said with a sigh. "For now."

* * *

Following Yukito's clean bill of health, he was discharged. But he stayed around to look after Sakura while Franklin and Touya went to work. Xiaolang arrived not long after Touya's departure, saving him the confrontation with Sakura's neurotic older brother. Tomoyo's grin widened as the Chinese boy entered, having noticed his every micro-expression of fear and concern.

"Are you alright?" he asked in the most nonchalant way.

"I'm fine, Xiaolang," said Sakura, eying Tomoyo's smile.

Oh, that's a nice look, she thought. She pursed her lips to conceal her joy. *I'm so glad Tomoyo is getting close to someone.*

"Lee, could you close the door?" asked Yukito.

The door to the room clanged shut and Kero finally popped out of Tomoyo's bag with a gasp. He panted heavily, his fur matted with sweat, before he suddenly charged into Sakura's face and hugged her head.

"My Master!" he cried.

Sakura wrenched him away and snapped, "Stop trying to suffocate me!"

"But you almost died again!" cried Kero. "Then, how'd I get all my sweets?"

Sakura's eyes narrowed while everyone else rolled their eyes.

"So all you care about is the sweets?" she mumbled.

Kero seemed not to have noticed her annoyed look as he clenched his fists angrily.

"That damned water," he snarled. "It got me and I couldn't do a thing. You almost drowned because of me not havin' my mojo."

"Us too," said Yukito. He pursed his lips with concern as he gazed at Sakura. "Show them."

Tomoyo handed Sakura her backpack. She procured the Book of Sakura (she felt weird calling it that) and withdrew the newly transformed Card. Its surface sparkled in holographic shades, diffracting the cold hospital lights.

"When I was hanging there," she began, holding up the key around her neck. "I realised that the Shadow Key wasn't the same, so I'd need a different incantation to activate it. I made one up, and it worked." She recited her new incantation, and the key transformed into her new wand.

Tomoyo clapped her hands together with excitement. "It's not the Sealing Staff anymore. It's a Star Wand!"

Sakura just knew her friend was concocting even more video ideas. She paid it little mind and moved on. She took one of the old Clow Cards from the deck and tapped it to the wand. Nothing happened.

"The old Cards still don't work," said Xiaolang.

"I feel like the book and the wand were telling me what I needed to do, so I came up with another spell to transform Watery into this new Card, Aqua," Sakura explained, holding up the sparkling Aqua Card. "And this one, I can feel is warm."

Kero held his hands up to it and his fur glimmered.

"Yeah, I can resonate with this one," he said. "So, new book, new wand ... meanin' new Cards."

"It sounds like you've created an entirely new Card using a Clow Card as a base," said Yukito. "A *Sakura* Card, if you will."

Xiaolang gave an interested hum. "Explains why you passed out."

"How?" asked Sakura.

"Clow Cards have a tremendous amount of magical power," said Xiaolang. "Using an inert one as a base would require an equal amount of strength. It'd be exhausting."

Sakura eyed the other Cards nervously.

"I don't like that I can't sense the Cards anymore," she said. "How about I do it all in one go?"

"No!" snapped Kero. "If one Card knocked you out cold, imagine what doin' all of 'em would do to ya."

"It could kill you," cried Tomoyo.

"That's right," said Yukito. "You should wait for something like that rain. Wait for a time when you actually need the Card, because then you'll have enough power to survive it."

Sakura wrung her hands with worry. "But I —"

"The Cards ain't goin' nowhere," said Kero, patting

Sakura on the head. "You got all the time in the world to change 'em. They'll be ready when ya need 'em, right?"

Tomoyo grabbed her hand and exclaimed, "That's right. And so are we!"

Sakura smiled warmly. "Thank you."

Tomoyo's eyes started to glimmer. "Plus! You now can wear my next generation costumes!" Out came the enthusiastic girl's sketch book, full of designs including a frog suit, a ballerina angel, and even a white leotard with a blue sailor's collar and matching skirt. She went on a fast-paced tirade of all her plans and concepts.

Sakura quickly gave up on following and cringed with excited dismay.

* * *

Sakura was held at hospital overnight for observation. Visiting hours finished and everyone had to push off. Kero hid in Tomoyo's purse, and his head hung over the edge of her bag with a perturbed look. It was the same one Xiaolang and Yukito wore, and Tomoyo could very clearly see it.

"You lied to her, didn't you?" she said flatly.

The boys stopped dead in their tracks and glared at her.

"She dun't need to know, Tomoyo," said Kero.

"Know what?" asked Xiaolang sarcastically. "That she *doesn't* have all the time in the world?"

"What does that mean?" asked Tomoyo.

"The Cards've got a deadline now," said Kero solemnly. "If she doesn't change them in time, they'll eventually die and vanish."

Tomoyo gasped, while Xiaolang fumed.

"I should've told her," he growled.

"Weren't you listening, Lee?" asked Yukito. "If we tell her, she'll try to change them all, and she'll die." Xiaolang's lips pursed tightly to contain his frustration. "I don't like lying to her either, but it's for her own good."

Xiaolang gazed back at the hospital, marvelling at the

oblivious girl sleeping therein. His body trembled with worry. He let out a low snarl to release his frustration, and then kept walking down the path. Tomoyo followed, trying to hold back her tears of concern.

Kero gazed over at Yukito, and called out through the resonance link. In the void, his winged lion form stood before Yue.

"Yue," said his mind. "Sakura's senses ain't tuned in yet. But yours and mine are. You gotta have sensed it too."

Kero saw fear in Yue's face for the first time in a long while.

"Clow was there that night," mumbled Yue.

5 | The Wing-Chun Marionette

The week following Sakura's accident was mostly uneventful. Her friends at school were obviously worried, but once they saw everything was fine, life went back to normal. Takeshi continued to make up fibs, and Chiharu punished him for them. Naoko pitched ideas for her writer's club projects, while Tomoyo plotted her next Cardcaptor video.

And Sakura remained cheerful.

There wasn't much else she could do. There hadn't been any strange occurrences that warranted the use of magic. Kero kept giving her the same pep-talk every morning.

"Ya gotta be cheerful and happy, ya dig?" he'd always say.

It never failed to make her smile.

One day, as Sakura enjoyed lunch in the schoolyard with her friends, she brought out a box of cookies she had made the previous day. Everyone hoed into the sweets, which put delighted smiles on their faces.

"Sakura, these cookies are delicious!" exclaimed Chiharu.

"Thanks," replied Sakura. "It was hard, though. Kero kept trying to steal them."

Naoko frowned. "What do you mean? That plush toy?"

Sakura almost had three simultaneous heart attacks.

Before she could freak out, Tomoyo butt in.

"She's talking about the video we made while baking the cookies," she said. "I'm working on CG-ing Kero into the video."

The others let out a long 'oh,' and reached for more cookies. Sakura glanced at Tomoyo and gave a look of dismayed gratitude.

Now, we have to make another video, she thought. *Oh well, I'll give some to Yukito. He's got a big appetite.*

"You'll have to show me how to make these cookies," said Chiharu. "Takeshi's birthday is coming up, and these'll be really good."

"What do you plan to give him?" asked Tomoyo.

Usually, Chiharu had trouble thinking of presents for her boyfriend. Today, however, she smiled and quickly replied, "I'm going to make him a shisa pair."

"Oh, now *that* is a good idea!" exclaimed Naoko.

Tomoyo chuckled excitedly, while Sakura frowned with confusion.

"What's a ssshisa?" she asked.

Chiharu grabbed her phone and showed them pictures of a pair of figures, hand-made from clay and painted in bright shades of orange and blue.

"They're from Okinawa," she said. "They're little lion figures. They say if you make a pair, and give one to your Number One and keep the other, then you're sure to be happy together for the rest of your lives."

Naoko and Tomoyo were amazed, and pressed Chiharu for more details.

Meanwhile, Sakura fell silent, and thought of Yukito. The sound of Elvin Bishop's 'Fooled Around and Fell in Love' echoed in her mind palace, in which she danced with Yukito. A pale blue tuxedo, glimmering in manifold colours, adorned his handsome physique. He twirled her, making her heart flutter with excitement. She procured a pair of lion figures, crafted from her own deft hands, and handed one to Yukito. He accepted it graciously, his eyes glued to hers. Then he took a knee, and Sakura's heart started thumping with trepidation.

"I will!" she moaned.

"Will what?" asked a voice that was certainly not Yukito.

Sakura's eyes flew open to find everyone looking at her with very confused expressions. Chiharu and Naoko asked if she was all right, while Tomoyo was clearly being strangled by stifled laughter. Sakura quickly shrugged off the red hue on her face, and downed the rest of her drink. She cursed Tomoyo for continuing to giggle while Naoko and Chiharu went back to talking about shisa.

None of them noticed the Chinese boy in the trees nearby. Xiaolang's highly trained ears allowed him to hear the whole conversation. His eyes locked on Sakura as he thought about Chiharu's prediction.

Happy together for the rest of your lives, he thought.

"Spying on girls ain't good, aye?" said a man with a thick Scottish accent. Xiaolang looked down and saw Eriol, a wide grin on his face. Xiaolang sneered at the substitute teacher, which made Eriol chuckle even more. "Ah, what a horrible face. Whatever did I do to you, Mister Lee?"

"Nothing," said Xiaolang. "Plus, if it isn't good, you shouldn't be spying either. Aren't you a teacher?"

"Eh, I'm learning," replied Eriol, his gaze directed to Sakura. "Lovely lady, aye?" Xiaolang's jaw clenched audibly. "She's already taught me a lot of Japanese. Maybe you can teach me some Cantonese?"

Xiaolang leapt off his perch and snarled, "Go to Hell." He then stomped away.

Eriol watched the boy, a pensive smile on his face.

"So *that's* what that feels like," he mumbled.

* * *

Sakura sat beside Chiharu and Tomoyo, on the way to Sekaido, the most popular arts and crafts store in Shinjuku.

It hadn't been the first time, since Tomoyo routinely dragged her along to see how different coloured fabrics looked on her. But this was the first time that she, the very much not artsy Sakura Kinomoto, was going to buy something.

"It's called 'fimo,'" Chiharu explained. "It's like clay, but you can bake it in your oven at home, instead of a kiln."

"I tried that once or twice," said Tomoyo. "But it was so hard to mould and sculpt, so I kinda gave up on it."

"Oh, they have softeners for it now," said Chiharu. She brandished a necklace that appeared to be made from jade. "I made this by mixing up a bunch of colours, and then after baking it, I sanded it down and smoothed it."

Sakura's eyes bugged out.

"That's amazing, Chiharu," she exclaimed.

"It was my first time I actually got it right," Chiharu shrugged. She eyed the chain around Sakura's neck. "It's weird, though. I always thought you'd used fimo to make your Shadow Key prop for your videos." She reached over and drew the key out from under Sakura's shirt. "Hey, it's different now," she mumbled.

"Oh, yeah, we're working on a new series of videos," said Tomoyo, drawing attention from the flummoxed Sakura. "New series of videos, so we figured a new wand would be good too. But we sent the designs off to be 3D-printed."

"Ooooh," Chiharu's eyes lit up. "Maybe I should do that for Takeshi too."

"I wouldn't," said Tomoyo. "It was really expensive to print our designs. Wasn't it, Sakura?"

Sakura stammered, "Oh, yeah, not cheap at all! And plus, I think Yamazaki would like hand-made shisa way more."

Chiharu beamed at that.

It was a ten-minute walk from Shinjuku Station, during which Sakura quietly listened as Chiharu brainstormed colour schemes and designs with Tomoyo. Her mind was sawash with visions of Yukito receiving her lovingly made shisa figurines, which, of course, were perfect in every way possible. She blushed at the thought of Yukito's immediate and forthcoming reciprocation upon her eloquent confession of undying love.

My dearest Yukito, she mentally rehearsed. *From the moment I laid eyes on you, I was truly enthralled by your amazingness! You're handsome, and kind, and smart, and gentlemanly! Truly any woman would be blessed to have you as a husband! Let it be me, for I love you beyond compare!*

It was emphatically *not* the first time she'd fantasised like this, and yet it just made her giddier and giddier every time she did it. By the time they reached Sekaido, Sakura's cheeks were the same mahogany colour as the large arches adorning the shopfront. Tomoyo had to lead her by the hand, because even a yell of her name couldn't break through her fantasy mode. She giggled and swooned as she trudged through the shop, mumbling Yukito's name over and over again.

Only once she'd collided headfirst with the sharp corner of a shelf did she finally snap out of it.

She rubbed her head, neurotically looking for blood in her hair, as she stood in front of the fimo shelves. She shook away her dizziness and looked at the products. There were so many colours, she quickly found herself baffled.

"I think I'll do glitter gold for the body, and caramel for the mane, tail, and ears," said Chiharu.

"Such a nice contrast," said Tomoyo.

"Well, not really," said Chiharu. "It's not really an artistic reason. It's just that his favourite sweet is taiyaki with chocolate filling. And he really likes it when the taiyaki is just the right golden colour."

Tomoyo turned to Sakura and asked, "What colours are you thinking?"

"Umm … I don't know," mumbled Sakura.

"Well, what kinds of things does he like?" asked Chiharu. "Say, what's his favourite food?"

Sakura pondered Yukito's voracious appetite. "He likes everything, I guess. He certainly *eats* everything."

"What's his favourite colour?" asked Chiharu.

An image of Yue's long silver hair came to mind.

"Silver, I suppose," said Sakura.

Chiharu hummed, rubbing her chin. Tomoyo, meanwhile, smiled pensively. The dark-haired girl finally spoke up.

"How about this?" she said, her finger raised. "Tsukishiro has light brown hair, and his name means 'White Moon.' How about you do one that has a glitter white body and a cognac mane? Then you can do one with a rosé coloured body and chestnut mane? One is you, and the other is him."

"That's excellent!" exclaimed Sakura, and she quickly grabbed fimo packs of the right colours.

The girls made their way to the counter, excited grins on their faces. Tomoyo and Chiharu chatted about plans to give the shisa to Takeshi, while Sakura meant to go back to her daydreaming. Before she could lose herself again, she noticed Xiaolang at the counter ahead of them. He finished paying and grabbed his purchase. Sakura could clearly see the packs of fimo through the plastic bag.

"Oh, Xiaolang," she exclaimed. "You're getting fimo too?"

Xiaolang stopped dead in his tracks. His face went pale when he saw her, and he stammered a string of gibberish, before finally blurting, "Yeah! Got a probem?"

"No," replied Sakura. "Are you making something?"

"Sshisa," he replied, before marching out of the shop. Chiharu frowned at the boy's rudeness, while Tomoyo chuckled.

Sakura grinned as she turned to her friends and said, "He must have someone he likes too." She did her best not to eye Tomoyo, but couldn't really help herself.

I hope Tomoyo accepts his feelings, she thought.

"Ah, when a lad's sweet on a lass," said a male voice behind them. The three turned and saw Eriol.

"Mister Lamperouge," said Tomoyo. "It's good to see you, sir."

"And you too," said Eriol, bowing politely. "It's a surprise seeing you ladies here so soon after school."

"We're getting fimo to make shisa," said Sakura.

"It's my boyfriend's birthday, so I want to make him something special," said Chiharu.

"Well, that's just grand," said Eriol.

"And you Eriol … er, I mean, Mister Lamperouge," said Sakura. "What are you buying?"

Eriol held out his plastic bag, which was full of different coloured thread spools. "Lots of holes in my socks, you see," he said. "Plus, my friend is doing a project involving a lot of string."

"Oooh," chimed the girls.

They paid for their products and sauntered out onto the streets. Eriol quickly took his leave, politely turning down Sakura's invitation to have coffee with them.

Chiharu scratched her head and mumbled, "Since when are you calling teachers by their first names, Sakura?"

"Oh, umm … since I speak English, I've been helping him with his Japanese," Sakura explained. "And he said it was ok to call him 'Eriol.'"

Chiharu pursed her lips, and gazed after the teacher as he turned a corner. She shrugged, "Well, it's not like he's in his forties or anything. We're almost his age anyway, so … Good for you, Sakura."

"What?" exclaimed Sakura. "I'm not … Eriol's not …"

Chiharu cracked a smile and laughed, "I'm messing with you. I know Tsukishiro's your Number One."

Sakura fumed the rest of the way home, any chance of reaching her Nirvana of Yukito blasted away. All she could think about was Eriol barging into any fantasy, heralded by Chiharu's salacious giggling. She got home, and completely forgot why she bought the fimo. It took a batch of Karaage á la Kinomoto, with a generous serving of kewpie mayo, to banish her bad mood. Luckily, she remembered to leave some for Franklin and Touya, as well as some for Kero, who was still playing *Breath of the Wild* in her room.

The thought of food brought her back to Yukito, and she remembered the fimo. She raced back up stairs with Kero's portion, and handed it to him, before upending the plastic bag on her desk and looking at the coloured contents.

Despite recalling the colour combinations suggested by Tomoyo, Sakura could not feel a tad of inspiration come to her. It didn't help that the fimo was really hard, just like Tomoyo had mentioned. She just stared at the blocks of clay for who-knows-how-long.

She jumped at the shock of Kero appearing beside her and mumbling, "Whacha got 'ere?"

"Fimo clay," said Sakura. "I was going to make a shisa pair for Yukito, but I can't get any inspiration."

"Get Tomoyo to make 'em," Kero yawned.

"No, I want to do this myself," said Sakura.

"Well, if it's for Snow-Rabbit, shouldn't ya got plenty of inspiration?" asked Kero.

Sakura eyed him. His comment made her feel vulnerable, and she grumbled, "Shouldn't you be playing your video games?"

"Meh, I'm takin' a break," said Kero. "C'mon, I'll help make 'em with ya, eh?"

Sakura sighed and set to work. After about half an hour, she'd finished forming the rosé-coloured clay into something resembling a body, but it wasn't nearly as amazing as she'd hoped.

"This looks terrible, Kero!" she exclaimed. "I'm not good at art."

"It looks fine to me, Sakura," said Kero as he stood beside the misshapen ball of clay. "Ya just gotta add the mane and it'll look just great!"

Sakura fumed. She reached for the lump of clay to continue working. Suddenly, her hand jerked, and a vision of a man in a star field tore through her mind. Kero's ears twitched and he gasped, "Clow!"

The pair scrambled to the window and extended their senses. They scanned the area, and zoned in on the strongest source of the magical signal.

"It's at Egota-no-Mori[1]," said Sakura.

"Call Tomoyo," snapped Kero.

* * *

A clear night sky hung over the park at Egota-no-Mori. Sakura gripped her Star Wand as she tried in vain to find the signature of Clow. Unfortunately, there was something far more distracting: a soft pink dress, a brighter pink tutu, and a flowery headband to top it all off. And Tomoyo would not stop swooning as she snapped photo after photo.

"Seriously, Tomoyo," Sakura groaned with embarrassment. "It's really important that I focus."

"Oh, but now I have the chance to catch Cardcaptor Sakura in more of my beautiful costumes," exclaimed Tomoyo.

Kero floated over with a flowery neckband that made him want to pose for the camera.

"C'mon, Sakura," he said. "Why d'ya think I said ta call her? So *I* can display my ungodly coolness!" And he let off a pose. A few clicks of the camera later, he drew his attention back to Sakura and bellowed, "That said, why'd ya invite Brat?"

Near Sakura stood Xiaolang, looking befuddled, and a little distracted by Sakura's costume. He managed to keep his attention on the conversation, and quickly retorted, "Because I might actually have some use here, Fluffy."

"Say that again, Brat?" growled Kero, his dukes raised.

---

[1]   A large park in Nakano Ward, Tokyo.

"Okay, alright, calm down," Sakura cooed. To Xiaolang, she said, "Thanks for coming. If it really is Clow I sensed, I wanted some backup."

"Where's Yue?" asked Xiaolang.

"Tsukishiro is at a part-time job with Touya," said Tomoyo. "He couldn't get away without making Touya suspicious."

"And that's the last thing I need," groaned Sakura as she pondered the horrible prospect of Touya learning her secret.

He'd make me do all the chores forever just to keep my secret, she thought.

Once more, the image of the cloaked figure in the star-field surged through Sakura's mind. She, Xiaolang, and Kero snapped to attention. Tomoyo fell into her silent spy mode as she captured their focused expressions.

With their minds, they reached out through the aether, searching for the source of the signal. And yet, even when they felt the signal stronger in one direction, it showed up from the opposite direction, until they realised it was all around them.

"Sakura, run," Xiaolang suddenly growled.

"Why? What do you sense?" asked Sakura.

"Just run, now," he yelled. He grit his teeth and clenched his fists, as if fighting against some terrible pain.

"What's the matter?" asked Sakura.

"I can't move," he replied.

His foot suddenly swung through the air, aiming for her head. Sakura only narrowly dodged the blow and she leapt backwards. Xiaolang kept on coming, swinging and punching and kicking. Kero assumed into his lion form, and lunged at the boy.

"What ya doin', Brat?" he growled.

"I can't control it," Xiaolang grunted as he threw Kero off him with ease. Kero fell onto his back, and couldn't recover in time to dodge Xiaolang's furious blows to his face and torso.

"Stop it!" cried Sakura as she tackled Xiaolang. The boy just kicked her off, and she tumbled across the park.

"Please, Sakura, just run!" cried Xiaolang. "I can't hold back any longer."

He started to charge her. She gripped her wand fretfully. Her legs knocked but she stood her ground. She procured her new Sakura Card, and prayed to it.

"Don't hurt him," she mumbled. Then she cast it out, "Aqua!"

A stream of water burst from her wand and buffeted Xiaolang. It didn't stop his advance, but it did reveal the thousands of threads that had somehow enthralled him. Sakura saw the threads, which reminded her of puppet strings, and she knew straightaway what to do. She held up the inert Sword Card and proclaimed:

Card of Clow, thy magic innate,
Discard thy form and reincarnate.
Ye serve, hence, under a new Master:
Sakura of the Shining Star!

With a flash, the Card shed its skin to reveal a new guise. Sakura touched the wand to it and said, "Free him from these bonds, Blade!"

The new Blade Card glimmered and transformed the Star Wand into a majestic star-speckled rapier. She gripped its hilt tightly as the sword took hold of her body and led her in an elegant dance through the forest of threads. She tore through the strings manipulating Xiaolang, until the boy was free amid a mess of wet thread.

Xiaolang fell to his knees and panted. Sakura edged toward him, to see if he was all right. She put her hand on his shoulder and murmured, "It's alright, Xiaolang. You were being controlled."

Xiaolang looked into her eyes and his fury softened under her gaze. But before he could respond, she fell into his lap, and was fast asleep.

6 | Fimo Shisa

Dreamlike hallucinations peppered Sakura's consciousness. At one point, Tomoyo was clutching her limp body and crying. At another instant, she felt as if her father was sitting beside her, calling the school to say she'd be absent. When she finally regained consciousness, she sat up. She was in bed wearing a clean set of pyjamas she didn't remember putting on.

"Wow, that was a deep sleep," she mumbled as she stretched.

"Ain't the first time, either," droned Kero as he floated over to her. His bleary eyes made her think he'd been playing video games all night. "I ain't done no games tonight. I been sittin' here makin' sure ya ok."

Sakura frowned, and turned to her alarm clock. It was almost two in the afternoon. She shrieked in alarm and raced to her wardrobe.

"Ya Dad already called the school for ya," said Kero as he averted his eyes from her hasty undressing.

"What do you mean?" asked Sakura.

"Ya couldn't get up, dummy," said Kero, his eyes shut tightly. "Ya been so tired this mornin', so he gave ya the day off."

Sakura's panic subsided and she smiled at her father's kindness. She changed into a set of normal clothes and sat down at her desk. The two transformed Sakura Cards glimmered in the afternoon light. She touched the new Card and ran her hand along its embossed surface. It appeared far more majestic and glamorous than the Clow Card it had been. Even the nameplate, 'Blade,' had an appealing texture to it.

"I can sense these ones now," she said. She reached out through the resonance link and felt their active forms.

"Them've been renewed," said Kero. He noticed her eyes fixed on the rest of the inert Cards, and placed his paw on her hand. "Don't worry. Ya'll get chances to change them too."

Sakura eyed him nervously, and gave a half-hearted hum of agreement. Since both Touya and Franklin seemed to be out at school and work, Sakura had the house to herself. She took the chance to finish off any outstanding homework, and then returned to her fimo sculpture. With Kero's help, she managed to make the rosé-coloured figurine at least partly presentable.

Then she worked on the glitter-white figure. She moulded, pressed, and manipulated the mass. Unfortunately, when she'd finished applying the cognac mane, it looked nothing like what she wanted.

"Sakura, it's fine," exclaimed Kero as he led her down to the kitchen. The flummoxed girl reluctantly put her sculptures onto a tray while Kero preheated the oven. Then they popped the tray inside and set the alarm for half an hour.

By then it was close to four-thirty. Sakura heard a knock on the door. Tomoyo and Xiaolang stood in the doorway. Their worried expressions vanished when they saw her smiling face.

They make a cute couple, thought Sakura.

"We just wanted to see if you're alright," asked Tomoyo.

"I'm fine, Tomoyo," chirped Sakura. She invited them in, but Xiaolang stood motionless.

"This is the first time being in your house," he

stammered.

"Please, come in," said Sakura warmly.

Xiaolang crept into the house and followed the girls into the living room. Sakura made them tea and laid out some sweets that were inevitably devoured by Kero. Tomoyo went on her usual spiel about the amazing footage she took from the previous night. Sakura was also impressed; Xiaolang, not so much.

The boy stood up and prostrated before Sakura.

"Please, forgive me for hitting you," he proclaimed.

Sakura sat flabbergasted.

"Xiaolang, that's not really necessary," she said.

"Yes, it is," said the boy, not raising his forehead from the floor. "I almost hurt you severely."

Kero harrumphed. "Nonsense! Ya apologise now, but tonnes of times ya almost *killed* Sakura. No apologies then?"

Xiaolang sat up and glared at the Beast of the Seal.

"The first time, I thought she'd fail the Final Judgement and I wanted to prevent the calamity," said Xiaolang. "The other times was to train her, like she asked. I wasn't using my full strength then. But last night –" He grit his teeth furiously. "Whatever those strings were, they were making me try to hurt her, with my full power." He looked at Sakura and threw his head to the floor again. "Please, forgive me!"

Xiaolang was motionless a moment, before a pair of hands lifted him up by the shoulders. Sakura put her arms around him and said, "Of course, I forgive you."

Xiaolang trembled in her embrace, and his arms started to reciprocate. His hands were halfway up her back, when they heard a soft, high-pitched wail. They looked at Tomoyo, her camcorder capturing their touching moment, one glimmering frame at a time.

"This is so cute," she chirped.

Beside her, Kero looked like he was about to burst a blood vessel. He growled, "Oi, Brat! Try to cop a feel and

I'll strangle ya!"

At that, Sakura pushed away from Xiaolang and shook with embarrassment. That shyness devolved into anger at her guardian, and she growled, "I hugged him, Kero! Don't be dirty!"

Meanwhile, Tomoyo just chuckled. She looked at a very nervous Xiaolang and mimed, "Love rival!"

Xiaolang's eyes narrowed and he thought, *This girl's sadistic.*

At that, the oven alarm rang, and Sakura's foul mood for Kero disappeared. She delightfully shrieked, "My models are finished!"

The others followed her into the kitchen and watched her giddily pull the tray from the oven. The two shisa hadn't changed much from the poses Sakura had left them in. As she set them down, she could see the glossy finish across their baked surfaces. Tomoyo looked up from her camera display and cried, "Aren't they adorable?"

Sakura's body trembled with excitement. She beamed at her friend, while Kero floated about taking credit for the success.

Xiaolang gave a gauche smile and said, "They look really good. You're really artistic, Sakura."

Before Sakura could thank him for the complement, Tomoyo quickly yelled, "You have to give them to Tsukishiro tonight?" She raced into the living room and fetched the paper bag she'd brought to the house. Her eyes glimmered as she proclaimed, "But first, you must be properly dressed!"

* * *

An hour later, Sakura stood in a pretty, pink, long-sleeved dress. Her body was shaking like a meteor had struck the Earth right beneath her feet. She could hardly control her legs as she willed them to carry her to the front door of Yukito's house. Her shisa figurines, cooled and cleaned, sat in a paper bag. Her nerves had driven her to crinkle the bag as she approached the house.

Tomoyo, Kero, and Xiaolang watched from behind the large tree in Yukito's front hard. Tomoyo, ever the manic paparazza, had her best camera fixated upon the girl. She was so excited that she could hardly keep quiet.

Kero was equally excited, and whispered into the camera's microphone. He made a voice as if he were narrating a nature documentary.

"Here we have the stereotypical magic girl," he mumbled. "Once thought to be purely the realm of shoujo manga[2], this elusive species is finally being observed in its natural habitat: the front yard of the love interest. This is truly a sight to behold."

Xiaolang gagged him and growled, "You shouldn't be making fun of her. She's nervous enough. Now be quiet."

Kero kept his mouth shut as Sakura reached the front door. She knocked timidly at first, and then more forcefully. She was a nervous wreck. Her brow was damp, and she was certain that her makeup was running in her sweat.

The door opened with a creak to reveal Yukito. He blinked away what appeareds to be sleep dust and looked at his guest.

"Sakura," he said, his eyes wide with surprise. "What can I do for you at this hour?"

Sakura didn't respond at first. She just crumpled the paper bag even more. A chorus of Utada Hikaru, Bill Medley, Jennifer Warnes, and Mamoru Miyano burst through her brain. She could barely bring herself to look up into her beloved's eyes, knowing what she wanted to say.

"Sakura?" Yukito repeated. "Is everything alright?"

"Iwanabrigyusoffingdhopyulikcuzmademysef!" she blurted.

Behind the tree, the trio face-palmed.

---

[2] Japanese: "girl's comic book"

"Sorry, you might have to repeat that," replied Yukito, scratching his head.

"I wanted to bring you something that I made myself," stammered the flummoxed girl. "I hope you like it!" And she thrust the paper bag at him. Bewildered, the boy reached out to take the gift.

A sensation suddenly ripped through Sakura's frustrated consciousness. It blew away every single feeling in her head and left only one thought. That same thought made Yukito gasp, "Clow!"

The paper bag dropped to the ground and burst open. A white and brown creature leapt from within the bag, and its jaws vectored for Sakura's head. The girl saw a flash of golden fur blast past her field of view, and she fell flat on her back. She looked over in a daze, and saw Kero in his lion form, wrestling with a white lion with a brown mane.

But, that lion looks all wonky and glossy, said her befuddled mind.

With a snarl, Kero bared his fangs and clamped down on the strange creature. In the next instant, the lion howled, "Gah! My teeth!" The creature swiped at his face and knocked him out cold.

In a flash of light, Yukito transformed into Yue. He unleashed a barrage of blue bolts at the creature, which dinged harmlessly off its solid carapace. The creature ignored him and charged Sakura. The girl clenched her eyelids shut in anticipation of a vicious mauling, but heard Xiaolang's voice bellow, "Run!" She opened her eyes and saw the Chinese boy before her, his hands emitting his magical shield against the wild monster.

Sakura's confusion immobilised her. Yue swept in on his wings and scooped her up. He carried her into the air and out of harms way. His Master in his arms, Yue floated above the front yard of Yukito's house. Sakura watched as Xiaolang wrestled with the creature.

"It's my shisa!" she cried. "Somehow, my shisa's gotten big and come alive."

"This is Clow's magic," growled Yue. Sakura realised her guardian was panting heavily, and sporting bags under his eyes. Before she could say anything, Yue suddenly fainted, and they fell to the ground.

Panic spurred Sakura into action, and she unleashed the Star Wand. She quickly drew the Wood Card and uttered her transformation incantation. She held her wand out to the new Card and proclaimed, "Make a bed for our soft landing, Forest!"

The branches from Yukito's tree promptly swept out to catch the two of them and deliver them softly to the ground. Tomoyo scrambled over to them and nursed Yue, while Sakura turned to the beast.

Xiaolang threw the creature off him and threw a paper charm at it. His fingers outstretched, he bellowed, "*Léidì zhāolái!*"

A flash of lightning engulfed the beast, which didn't bat an eye as it resumed its charge. Its head came very close to Xiaolang's stomach, but the boy managed to dodge it in time. He tumbled to the side as the beast came after Sakura. The girl gripped her wand as time slowed down. Her mind churned with a dozen thoughts about the creature and its nature. She considered its composition, which Kero couldn't bite, nor could Yue shoot. Lightning even passed through it harmlessly.

An image of Alice Axilotl flashed in her mind. Sakura grinned as a plan came to her.

She darted out of the way of the charging beast and raced down the street. The beast growled and gave chase. Then Sakura swivelled and drew the Earth Card. She gazed at the majestic woman emblazoned on its cold surface and she uttered to it:

Card of Clow, thy magic innate,
Discard thy form and reincarnate.
Ye serve, hence, under a new Master:
Sakura of the Shining Star!

The Card shed its form with a sparkle. Sakura touched her wand to it and proclaimed, "Sunder this effigy of faux stone, Gaia!"

Flurries of red and green burst from the Card and spiralled about each other. The helix consumed the charging creature and disintegrated it. The remaining shards clattered to the ground and shrank to a fraction of their size.

Sakura pocketed the new Gaia and Forest Cards and approached the inert pieces of baked fimo. The figurine's form was completely lost in the mess of a million pieces. Sakura edged her shaking hands toward the pile of dust, which started to waft away in the evening breeze. Be it the fatigue or the grief, Sakura didn't notice her friends approaching from down the street. She finally came to her senses when Tomoyo shook her.

"You changed two Cards at once," said Xiaolang. "How do you feel?"

Sakura looked up at them, her eyes two big waterfalls. She sniffled and sobbed at the sight of the obliterated shisa figurine.

"I worked so hard on it," she cried. She saw Yukito approach and quickly raced to dry her eyes.

Yukito smiled warmly and said, "Was that a figurine you made for me?" Sakura nodded. "Thank you, Sakura. I got a good look at it, and you clearly put a lot of thought into it. You're very artistic, you know?"

Sakura beamed.

"Oi," droned a voice. Kero, in his teddy-bear form, floated haphazardly over to the group. One half of his face had swelled into a big bruise and he looked really dizzy.

"Kero, are you alright?" Sakura exclaimed.

"I'm fine!" he yawped, before dropping out of the air and into his Master's waiting hands.

Yukito quickly led the group inside and fetched a bag of ice from the kitchen. Kero leaned on it like a pillow, and let out a long sigh.

"Last this happen'd was Kamagasaki[3]," he moaned. "Dang! That smarts!"

Sakura bowed and said, "I'm so sorry, Kero! I should have seen it and done something!"

Kero opened his tired eyes a crack and frowned. "Oi! You ain't snorin'. Ya just changed a Card, eh?"

"Two Cards," said Tomoyo. She brandished her camera. "And I have more footage for our next video!"

"Wow! Two Cards," exclaimed Kero, though it came out as less than enthusiastic. "Means ya gettin' stronger, eh! Ya gonna be super powerful soon."

"And so much more awesome!" swooned Tomoyo.

Yukito was much more pensive. He looked at Sakura, a serious look in his eyes, and said, "You sensed it too."

"Yes," said Sakura. "It was definitely Clow."

"But Clow Reed is dead, right?" said Xiaolang.

"Sure, he is," blurted Kero, his concussion clearing. "Me 'n' Yue watched it."

Yukito clenched his jaw as he glared at Kero. He sighed away the grief he shared with Yue, and continued, "But that was definitely his presence. So, if he is dead, then there's obviously someone trying to impersonate him. And that person must be causing these events to happen around Sakura."

"Maybe another Witch?" asked Tomoyo.

"Would have to be a very powerful one," said Xiaolang.

"Perhaps the same one that made Alice's serpent staff," Sakura suggested. "Did you learn more about that?"

Xiaolang gagged at the thought of that facsimile Sealing Staff.

"I'm still waiting on an analysis from my family back in Hong Kong," he said. "But I don't sense a Witch. I don't know what's going on here."

---

[3]   Location of a riot, on 1 August 1961, in response to the death of a labourer in a traffic accident.

Kero pulled himself to his feet. His face was still blue, and his balance was a little off, but he managed to keep himself upright.

"Whatever's goin' on, Sakura's handlin' it jus' fine, eh?" he said. "So far, ya've met the crazy stuff head-on, and won. No reason ta think ya won't get the next thing comin' ya way!" Sakura pursed her lips, a worried look on her face. Kero floated up to her and patted her head. "Never mind, eh? Ya got ya invincible spell."

Sakura drew a deep breath and said with a smile, "I'll definitely be alright."

Yukito led them to the front door to see them off for the night. Sakura's foot kicked against something on the ground, and she looked down to see the other shisa.

"Oh, Yukito!" she cried. She grabbed the pink figurine and held it up to him. "I made two of the shisa figurines. I was going to give you the other one."

"Oh, they're part of a set, are they?" he asked.

"I'll make another white and brown one," said Sakura. "But for now, you can hold onto this one."

"Are you sure?" asked Yukito. "Won't this one be lonely?"

Sakura shook her head. "She'll be waiting for her partner, and I'll make him as soon as possible. So, look after her for me, okay?"

Yukito beamed and stroked her fringe. "Thank you, Sakura."

Sakura's heart fluttered as she bade him good night, and then trotted after her friends. She immediately added more glitter white fimo to her shopping list. To her left, Kero and Tomoyo chuckled over the new footage, while Xiaolang was silent. She nudged him and said, "Thanks for having my back."

"No problem," replied Xiaolang.

Sakura thought of how he'd wrestled with that monster before. It brought back memories of the battle with Alice Axilotl, and how well Xiaolang had held himself against her. She knew he had a lot of martial arts training, which must have helped his magical strength.

Nothing ventured, nothing gained, she thought.

"Listen," she stammered. "Since things are getting a little dangerous now, there might be times where I can't rely on the Cards all the time. So, I was wondering ..."

"Yeah?" asked Xiaolang.

"Would you teach me kung-fu?" asked Sakura. "I figure, if I'm better at hand-to-hand combat, I'll be able to manage the Cards better." She turned to Tomoyo and Kero, who nodded in fervent agreement.

"Jus' so long as ya don't hurt her, Brat," said Kero.

"And *I* get to film it," said Tomoyo.

Xiaolang pursed his lips and thought a moment. His head tilted to and fro, before he finally said, "Sure."

7 | An Unexpected Casting

By mid-autumn, Touya had noticed Sakura disappearing every Saturday morning. She'd come back in the afternoon, visibly sore. He'd put two and two together after recognising a certain vexing caller ID on his sister's phone.

"Oi, what ya doin' with that creep?" he asked one morning over breakfast.

"Xiaolang's not a creep!" retorted Sakura for the millionth time.

Franklin swallowed a mouthful of tea and said, "And when am I going to meet this little boyfriend of yours?"

Sakura fumed. "He's not my boyfriend. He's just teaching me martial arts. That's all."

Franklin's eyebrows rose.

"Why are you learning that?" he asked.

"Well," Sakura stammered. "You see, Tomoyo wants to do more action scenes in our videos. And Xiaolang's good, so he offered to show me some moves."

Franklin grimaced. Images of his daughter being beaten up streamed through his mind. He reminded himself that his daughter was quite fit and could probably handle herself.

"Just be careful, alright?" he said reluctantly.

"Will do," chirped Sakura. She looked down to her pancakes, and her brain did a double take. She was sure she'd eaten her broccoli first, but there were three more pieces sitting on her plate. She glared at Touya.

"If you're gonna do wing-chun, ya need nutrients," the older boy snorted. He shovelled the rest onto her plate.

"You just don't like broccoli!" snapped Sakura.

Touya just snickered as he downed the rest of his pancakes. His sister fumed a little longer while their father chuckled. Sakura eventually finished her pancakes and left for her next training session. When she was gone, Touya sneered.

"I just hope she ain't shmoozin' with that creep," he muttered.

"Touya, don't be crude," chided Franklin. "Plus, Sakura's a smart girl. She knows not to spend time with uncouth boys."

"I know, I know," droned Touya. He looked to where Sakura had been sitting. His mother's ghost now sat there, and she nodded in agreement with her oblivious husband.

With a sigh, Touya stood and bussed his plate. Then he grabbed his bag and made off for work. He was actually quite excited for this job, thanks to the script in his backpack. Nadeshiko was really the one to thank, since she'd encouraged him to audition. He hopped on his motorcycle and sped down the street toward the city. He made a customary stop at Yukito's house, and let himself in the front door.

His heart skipped a beat upon seeing Yukito's motionless body on the floor. He sprinted forward and lifted him into his arms. He shook the pale boy and called his name, but received no response.

With a deep breath, Touya reached out with his mind. His soul trembled at the sensation of nothingness creeping upon his friend. Yukito's soul appeared like a two-pronged tree, withering in the absence of sun or rain, as venom invaded the ground beneath it. Terror filled Touya, and he screamed out through the aether.

Yukito woke with a start. He panted and groaned. He

shook his head to clear it and looked at his friend.

"Touya!" he exclaimed. His tone was as if he'd just been caught in the act of murder, and his voice shook with shame. "What's the matter?"

"What's the matter?" retorted Touya. "You fainted and I found you like this!"

Yukito's body trembled and he chuckled gauchely.

"I must've fainted," he said. "I've been really tired lately. I guess it just got the best of me."

Touya pursed his lips and glared at his friend.

"Touya, don't!" said his mother's ghost, but he ignored her.

"Yuki, this is wrong," he said. "You're fading, and I —"

"I'm fine, Touya," Yukito insisted.

"You're clearly not," retorted Touya. "And I know that you —"

Suddenly, Touya's phone rang. It was his boss at his new job, demanding to know where he was. With Touya distracted, Yukito sprang to his feet and dusted himself off.

"I'll make some tea," he said, leaving a frustrated Touya to his phone call.

Touya finished his call with the irate woman and followed his friend into the kitchen.

"Don't worry about tea," he said with a sigh. "I'm late for my new job."

"So you got the part, eh?" asked Yukito.

"Yep, I'm the Meiji-equivalent of Sherlock Holmes," replied Touya.

Yukito chuckled, "Too bad there's not a Watson."

Touya shrugged. An idea came to him and he quickly said, "Why don't you come with? Maybe they'll give you a part too."

Yukito blushed. "Oh, no. It's embarrassing enough that Sakura makes me participate in her videos."

Touya wouldn't take 'no' for an answer. He chided his friend and cajoled him to tag along.

Plus, it'll let me keep an eye on you, he thought. He did his best to ignore his mother's disapproving gaze.

Eventually, Yukito agreed.

* * *

Xiaolang stood in his living room, which had been completely emptied to make room for training. He tried his best to focus on the girl before him. Had he been alone with her, it wouldn't have been a problem. Disregarding the fact that she was the most beautiful girl alive (in his opinion), she was doing quite well in her wing-chun drills. Her fists were clenched and held on either side of her chest, her knees bent inwards, and she slowly descended and ascended on them.

Sakura completed her squats, and slowly extended her arms to assume the Wu Sau position. Her form was perfect.

"Ah! Simply wonderful!" cried a voice. It startled both of them and wrecked Sakura's focus.

Xiaolang turned to Tomoyo, who stood between three different tripod-mounted cameras with glimmering eyes.

"Daidouji, you're distracting her," said Xiaolang, suppressing his frustration. "Please be quiet."

"Sorry," said Tomoyo sheepishly.

Xiaolang turned back to Sakura and asked her to assume her position. He started with blocking drills, which Sakura had mastered quite well. He even felt comfortable with stepping up the pace of his blows, confident that she could handle them. She blocked each blow with one hand, just like he'd taught her. He grinned proudly at his pupil, who returned the smile amid her heavy panting.

"Gah! So cool!" shrieked Tomoyo. "I simply must make a training costume for you, Sakura!"

Sakura's focus disappeared again, and Xiaolang grew more annoyed. His eyes darted between his face-palming pupil and the irksome paparazza. The icing on the cake of utter irritation was Kero. The plush toy floated next to

Tomoyo and chomped on potato chips with the loudest crunch Xiaolang had heard.

His irritability reached the tipping point. He procured a paper charm from the pocket of his gym shorts, and growled, "*Fēnghuá zhāolái!*" A gust of wind scooped Kero, Tomoyo, and the cameras into the air and carried them to the door. Xiaolang glared down at the pair on the floor and proclaimed, "Sakura and I train alone from now on." And then, he slammed the door shut.

He ignored Kero's muffled protests and marched back into the living room. Sakura had her hands on her hips, and she did not look impressed.

"That wasn't nice, Xiaolang," she said sternly.

"I'm sorry, but it is just too distracting to have them here," said Xiaolang. "Why do you bring them every time?"

"Well, I don't want Tomoyo to feel left out," said Sakura. Her face reddened. "And I don't want her to think we're doing anything other than training."

"Why would she think that?" said Xiaolang.

"Well, it's just ... you and her," Sakura stammered.

Xiaolang choked. "She and I aren't —"

"No need to be shy," giggled Sakura. "It's nice that Tomoyo has someone."

Xiaolang's cheeks ran hot with both embarrassment and fury. He almost considered throwing her out as well, but decided against it when he beheld her captivating smile. He'd take on any embarrassing lie just to see her giggle that way.

Damn you, Mother, for showing me that photo, he cursed.

"Alright then, back to training," he chided. They resumed the blocking drills, but Sakura was evidently distracted. Xiaolang swatted her head to get her to focus, and her performance improved.

They moved on to Poon Sau drills for a while. Then Xiaolang decided to teach counters.

"This is a new position," he said. He beckoned her to

come at him. "Try and push me."

Sakura hesitated, and then lunged forward. Her palms contacted his chest. Instantly, Xiaolang grabbed her arms with one hand and held them tightly. With a simple press against her shoulder with his other hand, he pushed her to the floor. Of course, she was unhurt, as Xiaolang took care not to injure her. But she was pretty shocked.

"That's this is a good counter to a frontal push," said Xiaolang. He grabbed her forearms and put her palms against his chest. "Someone has you like this, you first grab with your left." He gripped her arms with his left hand. "Then you swing your elbow." He slowly swiped with his right elbow, carefully missing her face. "And then, thrust!" He pressed his elbow under her chin. Then he released her and stepped back. "Make sense?"

"Someone pushes me, grab, swing, thrust," said Sakura. "Not too hard."

"Shall we try it?" asked Xiaolang. Sakura nodded enthusiastically. Xiaolang hesitated. "Maybe I shouldn't have kicked Daidouji out," he stammered.

"Why?" asked Sakura.

"I can't push against *your* chest, can I?" replied Xiaolang nervously.

Sakura looked down and realised what he meant. She crumpled shyly and diverted her eyes. Her gaucheness gave way to a fit of giggles infectious enough to make Xiaolang laugh.

"Should I go and get her, so you can practice on her?" asked Xiaolang between chuckles.

"No, it's alright," said Sakura. "Just put your hands on my shoulders. That should be alright."

Xiaolang huffed, and gently placed his hands on her shoulders. In that moment, when he looked into her eyes, he felt the overwhelming urge to kiss her. Her sparkling eyes and upturned lips looked so inviting. Suddenly, he found himself on the floor.

"Oh, no! Xiaolang, I'm so sorry!" cried Sakura.

Xiaolang looked up at her in a daze. He gave her a dopey grin and said, "No, you did good! Excellent work!"

Just because I was distracted, he thought.

Sakura looked so happy with her success, once her guilt at hurting him had subsided. She practiced the manoeuvre a few more times, her proficiency improving even when he had greater focus. They trained for another hour, before Xiaolang decided they'd had enough for the day.

By then, they were both sweaty and the living room smelled like a gym. Xiaolang, ever the gentleman, let Sakura use the shower first, while he opened the windows and sprayed air freshener in every room.

"Umm … Xiaolang," Sakura called from the bathroom. "There isn't a towel in here."

"Oh, sorry," replied the boy.

He fetched a towel from the linen cupboard, and knocked on the bathroom door. He could hear the shower running, and a part of his brain with which he was seldom acquainted started nagging at him. It made a lot of very ungentlemanly suggestions to his conscious mind, which he suppressed.

"Sakura?" he called out. "I have the towel here."

"Just a sec," replied Sakura. The water stopped, and Xiaolang could hear some ruffling inside. His cheeks burned as he turned his back to the door and clamped his eyes shut. His skin broke out in goosebumps as the door opened. "Just pass it in here," said Sakura. He blindly reached around and offered the towel. He almost shrieked when her wet fingers brushed along his hand. The door shut, and Xiaolang bolted into the kitchen.

He completely lsot track of time, struggling to keep many an inappropriate image out of his mind. Steam seemed to rise from his head. He jumped three feet in the air when Sakura tapped him on the shoulder.

"What's the matter?" exclaimed the girl. "I called your name three times."

"I was just daydreaming," panted Xiaolang.

"Thinking about Tomoyo, eh?" giggled Sakura.

Xiaolang rolled his eyes and said, "Look, I was going to offer you some tea before you left."

"Oh, thanks, but I should be getting going," said Sakura. "I've got an school assignment I want to finish."

Xiaolang suppressed a disappointed sigh. "Well then, you'd better get going."

"I'll see you at school on Monday," Sakura chirped. "I'll make sure Tomoyo brings a lunch box for you."

The apartment door shut with a clack, and Xiaolang's ears rung with the sound of silence. He let out his dissatisfaction with a growl, and switched on the kettle.

Damn you, Mother, he thought.

* * *

Sakura trotted her way home. Her sore muscles hardly bothered her as she hopped along listening to her music. She meandered along the road toward Tomoyo's house.

Got better in training, and I didn't pass out when I changed two Cards, she thought. *Yep, thing's're goin' my way!*

"Don't lie to me!" growled a familiar voice from the adjacent street. Sakura was certain the voice belonged to Touya. She followed the sound to the front gate of a large mansion. She looked through the gate and saw Touya. He was ranting at someone whose face she couldn't see, and when he clenched his fist and threatened the man, she got really worried.

She summoned her wand, and held up the Jump Card. She uttered her incantation, and the Card transformed into a new 'Launch' Card. Wings appeared on her feet, and she leapt over the gate. She deactivated her wand and Card and scrambled across the courtyard to get a better look.

Touya now had the man by the throat, and he barked, "No more games, damn it! I know what you are!" He looked like he was about to strangle the man.

Sakura saw that it was Yukito. Horrified, she raced forward and tackled Touya.

"Leave him alone, you big bully!" she cried, throwing punches.

Bewildered, Touya struggled to push the distraught girl off him. It took Yukito and another man to pull her away.

"Sakura! Calm down!" cried Yukito.

"But he was choking you!" replied Sakura, tears near her eyes.

"Cut! Cut! Cut!" screeched a female voice. "Who the freaking Hell is this loony girl? Get her off my set!"

Sakura looked around to see cameras, microphones, and a film crew. She glanced at Touya, realising he was wearing Meiji-Era clothing and a really annoyed look.

"This is a film set, Kaiju," he said.

The director, a very irate woman with greying hair, charged onto the set and yelled incoherently at Sakura. The poor, befuddled, embarrassed girl could only murmur apologies. Touya appeared between her and the director and tried to defend her, but that just made the woman even angrier and she spat, "Fine then, Kinomoto! You're fired!"

Sakura's heart jumped into her throat and she shrieked, "You can't fire him! He did nothing wrong!"

"You're fired, now get the Hell off my set!" growled the woman, shoving and yelling. She charged at Sakura, and gave her a hard shove to the chest. Without a thought, Sakura grabbed the woman's arms with her left hand, swiftly brought her elbow across the woman's face, and then drove her into the ground.

The set was dead quiet.

A voice spoke up. It had a Scottish tinge to its vowels as it said, "Alright, everyone, calm down."

Sakura turned and saw Eriol. He was dressed so differently from his teacher's clothes, she hardly recognised him. He wore a pair of jeans and blue jumper that made him look respectable and casual at the same time. He walked over and helped the director to her feet, offering a smile to Sakura.

"I think it's unfair, Miss Director, to fire someone for something he can't control," he said with well-practiced Japanese. "I'm certain you don't mean it?"

The director stammered, "No. Not at all." She approached Touya, who straightened up. "You're not fired, Mister Kinomoto," said the director. "And ... your sister is welcome to watch, if she'd like." She then turned and barked orders to her production crew.

Yukito laughed incredulously. He turned to Sakura and exclaimed, "Girl, you've got some moves!"

Sakura responded with a shy chuckle. "Xiaolang taught me that today. And, I guess it just kicked in." She turned to Touya. "Since when are you in movies?"

"It's a part time job," Touya shrugged.

"He does it really well," said Yukito. He turned to Eriol and said, "Thanks for letting him be in the movie."

Sakura turned to her teacher and exclaimed, "*You're* making this movie?"

"Hee hee, nope, just producing it," said Eriol. "The director's father is a friend, you see. I'm also letting them use my house as a set."

Sakura finally took note of the mansion beside them. A blue-rooved house, it was fashioned in traditional European architecture. It looked like the castles Sakura dreamed of owning as a child.

Eriol turned to Touya and said, "You're doing really well, Mister Kinomoto. I guess acting talent runs in the family, eh?" He glanced back at Sakura, and made a face like a light had switched on in his head. He raced to the director and prised her over. He presented Sakura and said, "Won't she be good for the girl in scene fifteen?"

The director, her mood obviously improved, stroked her chin. She eyed Sakura up and down, making the girl feel very vulnerable. She turned to Eriol and murmured, "She can act, right?"

"Has her own YouTube channel," replied Eriol.

The director turned to Sakura and said, "You won't get

to do no kung-fu nonsense. But can you be in the movie?"
  Both Sakura and Touya shrieked in unison.

8 | Drama on Set

Tomoyo was the last person Sakura should have told about the movie. But she did, without thinking, and instantly was dragged into Tomoyo's fitting room for a new set of measurements.

"It's obvious that I would produce the costume!" exclaimed the girl.

"You don't even know what the movie's about," moaned Sakura as she was jerked this way and that for the various measurements.

"That doesn't matter," replied Tomoyo, a gleam in her eye. "I'll make a costume for every possible role in the Meiji Era!"

That night, Sakura had nightmares about being in a geisha costume.

Although Sakura agreed to be in the movie, the scenes involving her weren't to be shot for a few days. This left Tomoyo with plenty of time to read the script and actually make a proper costume for it. However, Sakura didn't put it past the girl to make a few dozen other costumes, just for the sake of it.

On the Friday afternoon before the filming, Xiaolang walked into Sakura's classroom. They were nearly finished with cleaning duty, so he waited patiently at the door, beside Tomoyo. He noted the slight lines of fatigue on her face.

"Sleeping much?" he asked.

"Costume-making overtime," said Tomoyo with a stifled yawn.

"Don't you have a van full of them?" asked Xiaolang. "Why do you need more?"

"Do you need to ask?" chirped Tomoyo as she brandished her camera. Xiaolang shook his head in dismay. The girl went on, "But there's also the big day tomorrow."

Xiaolang frowned. "What big day?"

"Oh? She didn't tell you?" asked Tomoyo. She quickly grabbed Xiaolang's wrist and dragged him into the classroom. Sakura was just finishing with the desk cleaning, and smiled when they approached.

And hand-in-hand too, she thought delightedly.

"Why didn't you tell Mister Lee about your debut movie?" exclaimed Tomoyo. "My dear Sakura's debut as a star!"

"Oh, sorry, it just slipped my mind," said Sakura. She explained the movie and how she ended up part of it. "So, the filming is tomorrow, and I won't be able to make training. Can we reschedule?"

"Should be fine," said Xiaolang. "How about Sunday?"

"Definitely," said Sakura. "Hey, why don't you come to the shoot? It'll be fun."

Xiaolang backed away politely. "No, thanks. I'm not that big on these kinds of things."

At that moment, Eriol passed by the classroom, and saw the friends chatting. He approached slowly, overhearing their discussion of the impending film shoot.

"Excited for tomorrow, Miss Kinomoto?" he asked.

"Of course, Mister Lamperouge," said Sakura. "Thanks so much for inviting me to be a part of it."

Tomoyo grabbed his hand graciously and exclaimed, "And permit me extend my deepest gratitude for the opportunity to craft Sakura's garments for this auspicious occasion!" Her formal speech put off the normally confident Eriol, and he could only catch a few words. He glanced at Sakura, who shrugged, "Too hard to translate into English."

Beside her, Xiaolang started to fume. He glared at the teacher and said, "This is *your* movie?"

"Oh, I'm just producing it," said Eriol with a wide smile.

Sakura started to explain, "He's doing it for a frie–"

"I'll go!" snapped the boy. "I'll go tomorrow! Got it?"

The blood drained from Sakura's face, and she squeaked, "Okay."

Eriol and Tomoyo fought to contain their laughter.

* * *

The day came. Sakura was so excited she'd hardly slept. She threw on a set of clothes, ate breakfast, and raced out the door with Touya. She was glad Kero didn't kick up a fuss about not being invited to the movie. He was still determined to finish all the downloadable content for *Breath of the Wild*, so he was content to hide in Sakura's bedroom all day.

She finally got to ride on the back of Touya's motorcycle. She'd been cajoling and begging and offering chore switches for months since he bought it. Now, he had to play nice and take her along. The moment Touya hit the gas, Sakura's stomach lurched, and she clung to his back for dear life. Every turn he made, Sakura made deals with God as her head neared the road. She eventually clamped her eyes shut and blocked out every sound.

They finally arrived at Eriol's mansion. Sakura leapt off the bike and raced away from the dreaded thing.

"You're the one who wanted to ride it, Kaiju," murmured Touya.

"I am never getting on that thing again," spat the trembling girl.

"Whatever," shrugged Touya.

Sakura gave a final shudder and turned toward the mansion. There was Tomoyo, waving excitedly at the front door beside Eriol. Next to her was Xiaolang, trying very hard not to glare at their English teacher. Before Sakura could run to them, she felt Touya's hand on her shoulder.

"What's that creep doing here?" he growled.

"Oh, Big Brother, leave him be," chided Sakura. "He's not going to attack me or anything."

She raced down the driveway to meet them. Tomoyo greeted her with tremendous excitement. Xiaolang's polite greeting was hampered by the presence of Eriol. Touya's warning stare did little to help.

Eriol led them into the house, where the film crew was preparing the various rooms for the scenes on their shot list. Touya departed to the men's change room to get ready for his scenes. Eriol led the group through the well-kept yet rustic house to the ladies' change room. Tomoyo immediately dragged Sakura into the room and slammed the door shut.

Having witnessed such an event before, Xiaolang quickly covered his ears. Eriol, however, could hear everything through the thin door. He pursed his lips with embarrassment upon hearing Sakura complain, "Tomoyo, let me get dressed myself!" and Tomoyo's curt reply, "Not enough time! I'll help you!" followed by repeated whines and protests from Sakura. The very uncomfortable Scotsman shuffled away, and leaned down to Xiaolang.

"Does this happen often?" he mumbled.

"Too often," murmured Xiaolang, his cheeks a deep red. He looked over and realised Eriol was very near to him. With a grunt, he shuffled away.

"Oh, have I offended you in some way?" asked Eriol. At first, his tone was facetious, but then he considered his words, and mumbled, "I didn't pooch my Japanese, did I?"

"Your Japanese is fine, Lamperouge," retorted Xiaolang in English. His American accent took Eriol off-guard.

"Oh, so you're from the States?" he asked.

"Hong Kong," said Xiaolang. "And *I've* noticed you

hanging around Sakura."

Eriol frowned, and cocked his head in confusion. A moment passed before Xiaolang's meaning finally dawned on him. Flummoxed, he exclaimed, "I haven't tried anything untoward, I swear!"

"See that you don't," spat Xiaolang.

Eriol nodded emphatically, and let out a long sigh. He waited a moment to let his embarrassment subside, and then said, "Sakura's really lucky she's got such protective friends, eh?" Xiaolang's lips up-turned slightly, which Eriol noticed. "Oh, wait a sec, laddie!" He looked really close at the Chinese boy's face, which turned away from him. Eriol started to laugh. "Ha! You fancy the quine!"

"Do not!" snapped Xiaolang.

"Oh, total pish!" retorted Eriol. Xiaolang crossed his arms tightly over his chest and scowled. "Don't worry, laddie. I won't blab."

If you do, I'll set you on fire, thought Xiaolang, his mind drifting to the roll of paper charms in his pocket.

The change room doors opened, and Sakura walked out. She wore a deep purple hakama[4] with iridescent floral patterns, over a bright pink haori[5]. She held her hands in front of her body and squirmed shyly like a newly-dressed bride. Xiaolang could barely look at her, thanks to Eriol making him all flustered. That same cursed Scotsman gave a supportive holler and applauded her arrival. The applause was infectious, and soon the whole crew was clapping and cheering.

"Thank you all," stammered Sakura.

Tomoyo held up the make-up bag and said, "We still have some preparations to make."

The director appeared and led them into the main living space, where the scene was being set-up. Sakura sat down and held still while Tomoyo applied the foundation to match the lighting of the scene. She soon moved onto

---

[4] A traditional style of Japanese trousers.
[5] A traditional style of Japanese jacket, typically worn over a kimono.

eyeliner, but realised she'd left the right pens in the dressing room and raced off. Sakura turned to Xiaolang and smiled.

"Thanks for coming around," she said.

"No problem," mumbled Xiaolang.

"I know it's not for me, though," said Sakura with a sly smile. "You just wanna hang around your Number One, right?"

"Number One?" choked Xiaolang. Sakura nodded in Tomoyo's direction, which made Xiaolang roll his eyes.

"Aye, don't we just love double-dates, eh?" chortled Eriol.

Xiaolang could have murdered him.

"Of course, Eriol!" exclaimed a very oblivious Sakura. "And I'm glad for Tomoyo."

"What about me?" asked Tomoyo as she returned from the dressing room.

"Never mind," said Sakura with a smirk.

Tomoyo started administering the eyeliner and mascara. She finished with a flourish and exclaimed, "Ah! My dear Sakura is simply divine! She'll light up Hollywood!"

Xiaolang let out an exaggerated sigh. Beside him, Eriol was being strangled by the need to laugh his head off.

"This is too good," he squeaked, just loud enough for only Xiaolang to hear. The Chinese boy started fantasising about all the ways in which he'd kill this wretched Scotsman.

Sakura shot up suddenly at the sound of a certain voice. In walked Yukito, in costume and ready for his take. He approached the group and complemented Tomoyo's excellent make-up and costume work. When Sakura said, "I'm so excited to be in this movie with you!" her eyes lit up with a sparkle to which Xiaolang and Tomoyo had grown all too accustomed.

Eriol absolutely lost it. His raucous cackles echoed through the house, disturbing the cast and crew. Sakura regarded the giggling Scotsman with a mix of concern and worry. She waited until the man had regained the ability to stand up straight.

"Are you alright, Eriol?" she asked.

"Oh, Sakura," moaned Eriol as he wiped away tears of merriment. He patted her head and said, "Your life is *so* fun! And you don't even realise it!" He walked up to Touya, gripped the boy's shoulders tightly and exclaimed, "Just *magic*, isn't it?"

Xiaolang needed to be out of the room, otherwise he'd be arrested for vicious homicide. Plus, he had a bone to pick with a certain paparazza. He grabbed Tomoyo by the wrist and said, "Can I talk privately a moment?" He didn't wait for a response, and dragged her out of the room. They reached an empty corridor, and he glared at her.

"Sakura has the wrong idea," he snapped.

"What ever do you mean?" asked Tomoyo, evidently loving the chaos as much as Eriol.

"I mean, she thinks that you and I are a couple," said Xiaolang.

"Oh, I see," said Tomoyo. "And you want me to set the record straight?"

"Please," snapped Xiaolang.

"Well, what better way to set it straight then to drag your supposed *girlfriend* off for a private chat?" quipped Tomoyo.

Xiaolang just glared at her. "You're worse than Lamperouge."

"Oh, don't blame me for this, Mister Lee," replied Tomoyo sassily. "In fact, I think the best way to set things straight is to tell her the truth."

Xiaolang inhaled nervously and gave a knee-jerk response. "Nope."

"Tell her how you feel," the girl insisted. "It'll make you feel so much better."

"She likes Tsukishiro, and I'm not taking that away," Xiaolang insisted.

Tomoyo scoffed, "That's no excuse. You're just a coward."

That pushed Xiaolang over a cliff he didn't even realise he was on. He thrust his finger at Tomoyo and snapped, "Whose the bigger coward?" Tomoyo looked perplexed. "If you're so keen on feelings getting out there, why don't *you* tell her how *you* feel?"

Tomoyo's heart seemed to stop. She clutched her hand over her chest and diverted her gaze.

"I don't know what you mean," she mumbled.

Xiaolang didn't let up. "Oh, I dunno, maybe that you want to take Sakura to Shunkou-in⁶?"

Tomoyo gripped her chest even tighter. She could barely meet Xiaolang's eyes as she murmured, "How long have you known?"

"The alleyway," said Xiaolang.

Tomoyo gave a dismayed chuckle. "Am I that obvious?"

"For God's sake, Daidouji, the only one who *doesn't* know is the magic girl out there," cried Xiaolang.

Tomoyo's eyes widened, and her breath caught in her throat. She coughed nervously and asked, "Even Yamazaki?"

* * *

Chiharu jumped slightly as Takeshi sneezed. She handed him a tissue from her bag.

"Someone must be talking about me," he sniffed.

"Hopefully only good things," said Chiharu warmly. She squeezed his hand and leaned on his shoulder. She took stock of her life, and that of her friends. She could only hope that they found someone they liked as much as she liked her Takeshi.

Especially Sakura, she thought. *Of course, she's got tonnes on her plate.*

---

6   Shinto temple in Kyoto that performs same-sex marriages.

"I wonder how Sakura's movie is going to go," she thought aloud.

"I'm sure Tomoyo will ensure it goes great," said Takeshi. Then he raised a finger. "Speaking of Tomoyo, you know about lesbians?"

Chiharu's heart sank into her stomach.

"Don't," she whispered.

Takeshi didn't hear her.

"'Lesbian' actually derives from 'elizbian,' as in Elizabeth the First," he explained, his grin widening. "That English queen never got married and had kids because she only liked girls. That's why any girl after her who only liked girls was called 'elizbian.' Eventually, that word turned into —"

Chiharu, her face blood-red, grabbed his collar and shook him furiously.

"We're on a crowded train, for Heaven's Sake!" she screeched.

* * *

"Especially, Yamazaki!" retorted Xiaolang.

Tomoyo couldn't reply. Her face was blood red with shame. Her mind kept swimming with images of her friends, and the realisation that they knew her feelings all along. Her stomach tied itself into knots at the thought. Then came the image of her mother.

"Look," stammered Xiaolang. She looked into his face, and saw remorse. "I didn't mean to upset you. I was in a bad mood and I shouldn't have said that. I'm sorry."

Tomoyo coughed. She wrapped her arms around herself and murmured, "I haven't even told my mother. I wonder if she knows."

"You'd hope she does," said Xiaolang.

"What do you mean?" asked Tomoyo.

"Well, think about it," said Xiaolang. "Your mother still treats you wonderfully and welcomed Sakura into her house. She welcomes *all* your friends. If she knows about you, and she still acts that way, it means she accepts you. Same goes for Mihara, Yanagisawa, and Yamazaki too."

Tomoyo's heart warmed at the notion. She beamed at the boy. She leaned in and kissed his cheek, earning a confused frown from the boy.

"I'll tell her that we're not a couple, so you'll have a chance," she said determinedly.

"A chance?" asked Xiaolang perplexed.

"You've got to tell her," Tomoyo stated flatly. "Anyone who can make someone feel better like you just did for me … You're more than worthy of her. Even more than Tsukishiro."

Xiaolang didn't know why. But, for some reason, receiving Tomoyo's blessing made him happier than he could remember. For a moment, he almost felt as if he had a chance.

9 | Grand Revelations

With a deep sigh, Sakura plopped onto a chair in the mansion courtyard. Her scenes took about three hours to shoot, and she was tired.

I'll never complain about Tomoyo's videos ever again, she thought.

Thankfully, her lines hadn't been too hard to memorise. And it was particularly easy to summon emotion for Yukito's character, being the elder brother of Sakura's character. Her only disappointment with the movie was that Yukito was playing the culprit. But she managed to use that to her advantage when shooting the confession scene.

Finally, it was all done.

"You look tired," said Tomoyo as she approached. Sakura looked at her, and found her expression somewhat different. The girl had her characteristic smile, but it seemed tainted by melancholy. At the same time, the girl looked a little taller, as if she'd been released of some burden.

"You okay?" asked Sakura.

"All good," said Tomoyo. "Are all your lines done?"

"Yep," replied Sakura.

"And wasn't she grand?" said Eriol, emerging from the house. "Congratulations, Sakura. You did really well."

"Thanks, Eriol," said Sakura with a bow.

"And thank you, Mister Lamperouge, for letting me make the costume," said Tomoyo.

"Well, they're shooting the big climax upstairs," said Eriol. He broke into English, "Fancy some snashters ss'n' tea while we wait?"

"That'd be brilliant," said Sakura. Eriol disappeared into the house. Tomoyo turned to her with a confused glance and Sakura said, "He's making some tea and sweets for us."

"Ah, very nice," said Tomoyo. Her voice was far softer than Sakura was accustomed.

"What's going on?" asked Sakura. "Did you and Xiaolang kiss?"

"No," said Tomoyo. "We're not like that."

Sakura rolled her eyes. "Tomoyo, you don't need to hide it. I can tell."

"You've got it wrong, Sakura," Tomoyo murmured.

"I see you smile at him all the time," Sakura insisted. "And, if me calling him 'Xiaolang' bothers you, I'll stop."

"I swear, I don't see him like that," replied Tomoyo. Beneath her calm façade, she grew frustrated. She saw Sakura open her mouth to speak, and her own lips moved of their own accord. "I like girls," she blurted.

Sakura froze.

"Come again," she said.

"I like girls," Tomoyo stammered after a long sigh. "I don't see Mister Lee or any boy like that. I never have really." She forced herself to keep eye contact with Sakura, who backed away ever-so-slightly. The girl's hand crept toward her stomach defensively.

"I see," she mumbled.

Tomoyo quickly said, "And there's a girl I like too. She doesn't go to our school. She's older. As in, Touya's age."

Sakura's eyes widened and she exclaimed, "Oh, God! So, you like older girls ... Like me." Tomoyo frowned. Sakura quickly blurted, "I mean ... I like older boys, and you like older girls ... So, like, as in *that*, we're the same, right?"

"I suppose," replied Tomoyo, finally breaking eye contact.

Sakura the bilingual seemed to have forgotten how to speak anything besides the language of stammers and babbles. Her fists clenched and her stomach tied itself into knots as she desperately sought something more to say to her friend. But, for reasons bizarre and unpalatable to her, all she could see was a stranger.

And her legs demanded that she run screaming.

A loud yell ripped through the awkward moment. Sakura heard it from the east-side balcony, and she raced around the house to investigate. Her heart stopped when she saw Yukito hanging from the balcony. Touya held his wrist and desperately screamed the boy's name, but Yukito didn't respond.

"He's unconscious," exclaimed Tomoyo.

I have to do something, thought Sakura.

Touya's grip started to slip.

Suddenly, the image of Nadeshiko raced through Sakura's consciousness, and she knew what to do. She activated the Star Wand, and drew the Windy Card from the pouch beneath her dress. She uttered her incantation and recreated the Card just in time. Touya's grip slipped and Yukito started to fall.

"Become a cushion, Gale," proclaimed Sakura.

A woman seemingly made of glass burst from the Card and flapped her wings. The flow of air raced upward to cushion the boy's fall and deliver him safely to the ground. Gale retook her Card form, and Sakura stowed both the Card and the Star Key beneath her costume.

She wasn't sure if it was the fatigue of changing the Card, Tomoyo's unexpected revelation, or the fear that Yukito might have died. But her body would not stop shaking. She couldn't even run to see if her Number One was all right.

* * *

Touya sat by his friend's bedside. His knuckles were white from clenching his costume, and his palms were sweaty. He could not shake the image of Yukito fainting and falling from the balcony. The image replayed over and over in his mind, and no matter how hard he tried, he could not change the outcome. It was as if his mind was taunting him for his powerlessness.

His heart skipped beats when he saw part of Yukito's body become translucent.

It had done the same thing before he fainted. It had happened many times before – far too many times.

Desperate, Touya reached forward to rouse him. Nadeshiko appeared from outside his vision, and grabbed his hand. His eyes met her horrified gaze and she said, "Don't."

"I have to," retorted Touya. "He'll die if I don't."

"Give her time, Touya," pleaded Nadeshiko. "She's getting stronger."

"Not fast enough," said the boy. He tried to wrestle his hand out of his mother's grip but she fought back. Touya's fury took hold of him and he pushed her toward the wall. Her ghostly form melded right through it, obscuring her face. Touya took a deep breath and stepped back. Nadeshiko emerged from within the wall, tears streaming down her face.

"You're the only one who can see me," she cried. "If you give your powers to him, I'll be watching you alone. Don't make me go through that."

Touya's shoulders slumped and he shook his head with dismay. Completely fed up, he asked a question he'd been dying to ask for a long time: "What are you even doing here, Mum? You're dead. Isn't there a fun afterlife where you can have a cosmo with Grandma?"

"And leave you three alone?" retorted the ghost. "There are things I need to do still. I *need* to be around you and Sakura."

Touya's eyes started to water. He sniffed back his tears

and said, "I need him."

Nadeshiko hiccoughed with grief. She made one last feeble attempt to stop her son, but he ignored her and roused Yukito. The boy was groggy at first, and it took time before he was able to sit up and speak.

"What happened?" he droned.

"You fainted again," said Touya, his voice shaky. "You fell off the balcony, but luckily you weren't hurt."

"I'm sorry," yawned Yukito. "I don't know why I'm so tired."

Touya grit his teeth, fed up with the obvious lies. He pulled Yukito so he could look straight into his friend's eyes. He opened his mouth to speak.

A sudden and loud rapping on the door heralded the director's arrival. The woman charged into the room and shouted, "Goddammit, are you awake yet? We need to get these shots finished before the end of the day."

Touya glared at her, his eyelids twitching with pure rage. He grabbed the cantankerous woman by the scruff of the neck and threw her out of the room.

"I need to talk to Yuki in private!" he yelled. "Back the Hell off!" And he slammed the door, and locked it. He leaned his back against it and breathed deeply to calm himself. He tried his best not to look at his mother's pleading gaze as he walked back to the bedside.

"Look, Touya, you're in a bad mood," Yukito began. "I promise I'll go to the hospital and find out why I'm fatigued."

"Cut the crap, already!" cried Touya. "All three of us know why you're sick."

Yukito's eyes widened with horror. Blood drained from his already pale face.

"What do you mean, all three of us?" he stammered.

"That other guy," said Touya. "You know, the Moon guy that hangs around Sakura?"

Yukito grit his teeth and growled, "I don't know what you're talking about."

Touya's face softened and he sat on the bed. He cupped his friend's cheek as gently as his shaking hands would allow. He spoke slowly and quietly.

"I know you're not human," he said. "I knew it straight away. So, stop hiding."

Yukito's surprise, smeared across his face, slowly gave way to resignation. He shed a single tear as silvery floes of energy started to swirl about him. They grew in size and brightness, until they completely enveloped him. They soon cleared, revealing the man Yukito had been hiding. Touya stood in front of him and eyed him up and down.

"You're shorter than I expected," he said with a smirk. "So, what do I call you?"

The ornately dressed man sneered, though his eyes radiated sadness.

"Yue," said the man. His lips trembled with the shared pain of his alter ego. "You were the last person he wanted to know."

"Well, tough," said Touya. "I needed to meet you."

"Why? To see all sides of him before he goes," asked Yue sarcastically. He had a look of a cynical person on death row.

"No," snapped Touya. "I needed to meet you so I could give my powers." Yue choked with surprise. "Sakura's ain't enough, right? That's why you're disappearing."

"She shouldn't have become Master of the Clow," said Yue.

"And yet you agreed, didn't you?" said Touya.

"It was by the will of Clow that it be so," replied Yue. "So, too, must my inevitable disappearance."

"Bullshit!" spat Touya. "If you disappear, so will Yuki. I don't want that. And if you disappear, who'd look after Sakura when I can't? Screw the will of some dead guy. I'll change it."

Yue raised an eyebrow. He gave a smirk of admiration for the boy in front of him, and gave his proposal some thought.

"You won't be able to see your mother anymore," he warned.

Touya sighed, "It's not fair that only I can see her. Plus, I'm sure she'd prefer you guarding her daughter, than whether or not she can talk to anyone."

His eyes darted to Nadeshiko's ghost, standing behind Yue. Her jaws tightened with sorrow, and yet she forced herself to nod in agreement. He looked back at Yue and thrust a finger in the shorter man's face.

"But this comes at a price, Moon Boy," he snapped. "You gotta guard that Kaiju with your life. You guard Yuki *with your life*, or – so help me, *Christ!* – I'll end your arse. Got it?"

Yue scoffed.

"It goes without saying," he replied.

Touya gave his mother one last glance, and she silently waved goodbye. Then, he embraced Yue. In an instant, his body started to drain of energy. Tremendous fatigue overtook him. The last thing he saw before fainting was his mother, fading from view.

Yue caught the unconscious boy and guided him to the bed. He stood erect and breathed deeply. He felt invigorated, and for once could sense beyond the confines of his body. He could sense the plasterboard and wooden chassis of the house, the paint on the walls, and the rustle of the grass outside. He could even sense the soft whimpers of someone at the door.

With a flick of his hand, Yue unlocked the door, which swung open to reveal Sakura. Her face was buried in her hands, and her body shook uncontrollably. Yue faltered with shock.

"You heard everything?" he asked.

Sakura looked up at Yue, her eyes red with tears. She charged across the room to the bed and grabbed her brother's hands.

"All because of me," she wailed. "He lost his powers,

all because of me."

"He gave them away willingly," said Yue.

"But it's my fault," said Sakura. "If I had been stronger, Yukito would've ..." She couldn't complete the sentence. She looked at Touya, unconscious on the bed. "All this time I thought he would have laughed and made me do chores to keep my secret. But he knew, all along. I don't even have the power to see my own family for what they are. How could I have enough power to keep my Number One alive?"

And she cried and cried.

A hand slid its way into hers and pulled her up. Yue made her stand up straight, and then he knelt before her.

"Even I lack that power, Master," he said, brushing away her tears. "I, like the Cards, am born of the magic of Clow Reed the Incomparable. It's obvious that a child like you would not be able to handle it alone."

"Then why did he choose me?" Sakura sobbed.

"Maybe because you're a kind person," said Yue. "I could see it myself during the Final Judgement. Also, it may be because you have people around you who will support you, like your brother. And because of them, you have a true capacity for joy." Yue did something Sakura hadn't seen him do before: smile. "You shouldn't cry," he said. "For his sake, you mustn't cry."

Sakura's emotions were like a horse that refused to be wrangled. She did everything she could to stop shaking, but the fight wasn't going her way. She grabbed Touya's hand and said, "I'll protect you."

* * *

Yukito stayed at the mansion with Touya, who slept for quite a while after. The rest of the filming was scheduled for a later date, and everyone packed up and went home.

Sakura walked home in silence beside Tomoyo and Xiaolang. The normally talkative Tomoyo was equally silent once Sakura had explained what had happened. The quiet eventually got to Xiaolang and he stammered, "I'm sorry for, you know, not noticing Tsukishiro's condition sooner. I should've been paying attention."

"It's fine," said Sakura. "I didn't see it either. And I'm much closer to Yukito than you are."

"You mustn't blame yourself, Sakura," said Tomoyo. "You're still getting the hang of the Cards. You'll get better at it, I'm sure."

Sakura's smile was half-hearted as she regarded Tomoyo. Combined with the painful cocktail of regret and dismay, she still felt a twinge of unfamiliarity with her best friend. It made her feel worse.

They finally reached her house, and she bade them goodnight. She quickly explained to Franklin what had happened, and then retreated to her room. She shrugged off her father's questions about her own mood, and locked the door behind her.

She had expected to see Kero, still pounding away at the Nintendo. Instead, she found him curled up in his apartment in her desk drawer. She was almost glad for it, since she didn't really feel like discussing the day's events a second time. Plus, she *really* didn't want to deal with Kero's reaction to Touya's knowledge.

If she was to be honest, she didn't want to deal with Kero, period.

She switched off her bedroom light, and lay down on her bed, clothes and all. Despite her fatigue, she couldn't sleep.

I almost lost him today, she thought. *I almost lost my Number One, and it happened right under my nose. And it could happen at any time.*

She thought about Tomoyo's revelation. Though it had off-put her tremendously, she had to admire her friend's courage.

*I need to be that brave. I can't leave something so important unsaid. That's why, tomorrow, I am going to Yukito's house, and I am going to tell him ... **everything**.*

10 | A Long-Coming Confession

The clock read eight in the morning. Sakura stood in front of the mirror, having only had a few hours of sleep. It didn't show much on her face, especially after a hot bath and moisturise. Her eyes blasted an air of confidence and determination at her reflection.

She blow-dried her hair, and styled it with her nicest hairpins. Then, she applied some foundation, blush, and perfume. She went into her bedroom, where Kero was still asleep. She found a yellow dress Tomoyo had made for her fifteenth birthday. That time, before she'd found the Book of Clow, seemed so long ago, almost in another life. She smiled as she ran her hands along its soft fabric.

Thank you, Tomoyo, for giving me this strength, she thought.

She donned the dress, and twirled in front of the mirror a few times. She drew a deep breath, and steeled her nerves.

"Let's do this," she said.

Sakura marched out of her bedroom and down the hall. She could hear Touya's snoring through his door, and smiled that he was all right, if only a little tired. His presence also told her Yukito was at home. She walked into the kitchen, where Franklin was cooking breakfast.

"Good morning," he said. He grinned at her appearance and said, "You're looking particularly lovely today. What's the occasion?"

"Oh, nothing," said Sakura with a coy smile. "I just felt like dressing nicely today."

And this afternoon, I'll surprise you with my engagement announcement, she thought giddily.

"Well, I'm glad to see you're alright," said Franklin as he served her some bacon and eggs. "Yesterday, you looked a little upset."

Sakura's grin widened. "I was just tired, and worried about Big Brother fainting."

"Well, Tsukishiro brought him home safely last night," said Franklin. "He looked very tired still, but he seems to be doing alright."

"Good," exclaimed Sakura as she grabbed a napkin and hung it from her collar. She ate her breakfast slowly, not wanting to burp at the crucial moment. Then, she bussed her plate, drank a glass of water, and kissed her father goodbye.

"I'm going out for a bit," she said over her shoulder.

It was a bright day, if a bit chilly thanks to the autumn season. The cherry blossom trees on her street were bare, but Sakura didn't mind. She breathed in the cool air, which soothed her ever-present nerves. She made each step down the street with trepidation, but also confidence.

Her new life was to start today.

Sakura turned down a few adjacent streets, wending a path she knew well, until she reached the house of one Yukito Tsukishiro. With a huff, she passed through the gate, marched through the front yard, and knocked on the door. She stood tall and with deference.

Her skin broke out in goosebumps as the door opened to reveal Yukito. He definitely looked much better than she'd seen him in a while. There was significantly more colour to his hair and cheeks, courtesy of Touya's sacrifice.

You gave me the time to take this chance, she thought. *Thank you, Big Brother Touya.*

"Good morning, Sakura," said Yukito warmly. He motioned for her to enter. The girl silently followed him through the hallway toward the kitchen. Her eyes were glued to him the entire time, despite her burning cheeks and her thumping heart.

"How's Touya?" asked Yukito.

"He's fine," said Sakura. "Still asleep, but doing good."

Yukito beamed. "We're both so grateful to him."

"So am I," said Sakura. Her mind frantically searched for the speech she'd prepared, and she froze upon drawing a blank.

"Well, how about a cup of tea?" asked Yukito.

Without any permission from her brain, Sakura caught Yukito's hand and gripped it tightly. She looked straight into his eyes, and fixated upon him.

"You almost disappeared," she said. "I almost lost someone very important to me. But thanks to Big Brother, I now have this chance." She felt as if her blood was boiling acid, and her stomach was a lump of ice. She huffed, pushing away the sheer terror that had gripped her.

Now or never, Sakura!

"I love you, Yukito Tsukishiro," she proclaimed. "I always have. From the minute I first saw you, I knew I wanted to marry you and be with you forever. You're my Number One."

Time stopped.

Nothing went on in Sakura's head for an incalculable eternity. All she saw was Yukito's face, right in front of her. His expression was inscrutable, even if Sakura's brain hadn't completely shutdown.

Time resumed when she felt his hand on her cheek.

Does he accept? Is he going to kiss me?

Yukito's thumb drew a line down her jaw, sweeping along her chin. But he didn't kiss her.

"Thank you, Sakura," he said. "That is very sweet."

"Then, do you ..." stammered Sakura.

Yukito released her hand, which fell limp to her side.

"I'm not worthy of you," he said.

Sakura's heart turned to ice.

Before she could respond, he silenced her. "Think about your feelings for your father and brother. Are your feelings for me different in anyway from them?"

Sakura started to feel dizzy. She closed her eyes and thought hard.

These feelings are nothing like how I feel about Big Brother, she thought mechanically. *Of course, I like Touya, but he's a meanie and plus, hello? Big Brother? Gross! And my Dad ... he nice, and kind, and supportive. If he had wings and magical powers, he'd defend me just like Yue would.*

Her eyes opened slowly.

Just ... like Yue ...

She looked back up at Yukito. No more could she feel giddiness at his presence, or the elation of hearing his voice. Confused, she glanced around his kitchen, and her eyes fell upon a crucifix hanging on the wall above his dining table.

"Are you Christian?" she blurted.

"Yeah," he chuckled.

I didn't know that, she internally screamed.

She thought back to when she was buying fimo to make her shisa.

I couldn't figure out what colours to make his shisa. Chiharu asked me what his favourite food is, and I had no idea. "He certainly eats everything!" **That** *was what I said? I don't even know what his favourite colour is. I guessed based on what Yue looks like. Come to think of it, I don't even know when his birthday is. I at least know that about Tomoyo, Big Brother, and Dad.*

"You're right," she whispered, her head hung in shame. "They *are* like Dad."

Yukito lifted her chin to look at her.

"You shouldn't be with me, Sakura," he said. "I would just get in the way of you finding your real Number One. It wouldn't be fair to you, or to me."

"To you?" Sakura droned.

"I already have my Number One," he said softly.

Defeat washed over Sakura a second time. A twinge of

jealousy ripped through her mind and she wondered who it was. She knew it had to be someone Yukito liked being around, but the only one she'd ever seen him with was Touya. An image of Tomoyo's vulnerable expression flashed through her mind, and the realisation struck her. It was almost comical, and she chuckled.

"It's Big Brother Touya, isn't it?" she asked. Yukito's surprised expression – an exact match to that of Tomoyo's confession-face – told her she was right.

"Yeah," said Yukito gauchely. "But I don't know if he feels the same way."

"Of course, he does, you dolt!" snapped Sakura, grinning maniacally. She grabbed his hands and said, "He definitely does. Why else would he have given away his magic, you big silly? And you should tell him too. He'll definitely say he likes you back. I'll bet my life on it!"

Yukito burst into a fit of laughter. "Your life, you say?"

"I'm good for it," she proclaimed. "And if Big Brother ever hurts you, tell me and I'll kick his bum!"

Yukito beamed and said, "Good to hear, Cardcaptor." He held out his hand and shook hers. "And if you find your Number One, and he hurts you, let me know, and Yue and I will kick his butt!"

"Deal!" exclaimed Sakura.

They laughed a little while longer. Fatigue started to grip Sakura and she sighed.

"I should get going," she said. "I've got some homework I want to finish. Also, I left Kero without any breakfast."

"Oooh, bad move," said Yukito, nervousness starting to come over him.

"Thanks for having me," said Sakura with a bow. "Sorry to intrude." She walked toward the front door, adrenaline pumping through her legs and demanding her swift flight. The back of her eyes stung, but she retained her composure.

"Oh, wait a minute," said Yukito. He raced into an

adjacent room, and came back with something in his hand. He placed it in Sakura's palm. "When you find your Number One, give him this," he said with a warm smile, the same that once intoxicated the girl. It was that smile that was, from now, forever beyond her reach.

Sakura looked down at her hand, and saw her pink shisa.

I didn't make another one for him, she thought. It felt like a final nail in the coffin.

She forced herself to bow politely and walk away slowly. When she was out of eyesight, she broke into a run that her fine shoes were not designed for. She tripped on some fallen leaves, and hit the asphalt. The fabric of her dress tore, and the front was scraped badly. She scrambled to her feet and powerwalked the rest of the way home.

Franklin had gone out and Touya was still asleep. But Sakura didn't notice. She went to her bedroom where Kero was playing his games again, wolfing down one of Sakura's signed puddings. She sat on the bed and wiped away the carefully applied makeup that was now streaked by her tears.

Kero turned and noticed the state of his Master. He switched off the TV and floated over to her.

"Sakura, what's the matter?" he asked. The girl just stared past him.

"Kero, am I an idiot?" asked Sakura.

"What the matter?" asked Kero.

"I must be an idiot," she whispered. "I notice nothing."

"Come on, Sakura, don't say that about yourself," said Kero.

Tears started to streak down Sakura's face and they wouldn't stop coming.

"I'm supposed to have magical powers but I mistook the Clow Cards for a book of novelty tarot cards. I'm supposed to be a good friend, but I couldn't see that Tomoyo likes girls. I'm supposed to be a good sister, but I didn't realise that Touya also has magical powers, can see

Mum, and knew about me being Cardcaptor from the very beginning. I mean, he *could* see her. He can't now, because while I'm supposed to be an all-powerful magician, I didn't notice that Yue was disappearing because of me not being strong enough. So Touya gave up his magical powers to keep Yukito from dying. I didn't even notice the love of my life disappearing before my eyes. I was supposed to love him so much and yet I didn't realise I hardly knew the guy, much less notice that he likes Touyas. Add to that how much of a horrible sister I am because I didn't realise that Touya was on to me from the beginning, looking out for me all along, *and* in love with the man I just arrogantly waltzed down the street to propose marriage to!"

Kero's eyes bugged out and his jaw hung loose in shock.

"Whadafaaajaga?" he stammered in fluent gibberish.

"I was afraid I'd wouldn't get a chance to tell him how I feel," Sakura went on. "I just wanted to be with him." She broke down. She gripped her trembling body tightly and cried. Kero tried to console her as best as he could, but she wouldn't stop rambling.

"Sakura, it's alright," he cooed. "So he turned you down, and so there are some things about your friends you didn't know. That doesn't make you a bad person, or an idiot." He tried to look at her face as she cried harder. "Sakura, look at me," he said firmly. She managed to open her red, puffy eyes. "You've done such an awesome job at being Cardcaptor," he said. "I saw you'd transformed Windy, and according to this new chick, Gale, you didn't even break a sweat. You're doing amazing. And if Snow-Rabbit doesn't feel the same way, you still get to be his friend. Cheer up, eh?"

There was a glimmer of desperation in Kero's eyes, and Sakura saw it through her veil of tears. She glanced at the Cards on her desk. Her heart skipping beats, she scrambled over and picked up the inert Cards.

"They feel colder than before," she snapped. "Why?"

Kero swallowed nervously. "I dunno."

"Don't lie to me, Kerberus," barked Sakura. "I've been failing my friends and family, left, right, and centre. I can't fail anymore. Why are they colder?"

Kero's face turned pale and he held his paws up. "Sakura, look, you're scared and you're sad. Just put the Cards down and relax."

His Master wouldn't have it.

"Two months ago, after I changed the first Card, you said I had all the time in the world," she said. "Do I?"

"Sakura," Kero pleaded.

Sakura's eyes flashed green. An unseen force threw Kero into the wall, and he felt his Master's voice penetrate the resonance link. A tremendous power, fuelled by grief, wormed its way past his mental barriers as if they were nothing, and laid his mind open. It found its answer, and withdrew in horror. Kero opened his eyes and saw Sakura, doubled-over and hyperventilating.

"They'll die," she gasped.

"Sakura, listen to me," Kero pleaded, but he was drained and could hardly move. His eyes widened in horror as Sakura summoned the Star Wand. Then, she held up the remaining eleven Cards and proclaimed:

> *Cards of Clow, thy magic innate,*
> *Discard thy forms and reincarnate.*
> *Ye serve, hence, under a new Master:*
> *Sakura of the Shining Star!*

Her wand activated with a roar, drowning out Kero's cries to stop. She held the wand to the Cards, and willed her every ounce of energy into them. Illusion became Maya; Flower became Bloom; Thunder turned to Spark. One by one they changed. Elation filled Sakura as quickly as her stamina drained. Yet she pressed on desperately, scraping the bottom of the barrel, until her legs gave out, and she collapsed.

Her heart stopped.

11 | Coma

On Monday, the sky was cloudless. The sun shone through the windows of Sakura's classroom, and struck the two empty seats at the back. The room, though filled with students, was deathly silent. The students' jaws hung wide open with shock and confusion.

"What did you just say?" exclaimed Chiharu.

The teacher cleared his throat and said, "It seems that Miss Kinomoto collapsed yesterday. Her elder brother found her in her bedroom, and called an ambulance. She was taken to hospital, where she remains unconscious."

"Have they determined what happened?" asked Takeshi, his voice unusually stern.

"Her father has explained that massive physical exhaustion caused her heart to stop," said the teacher. Terrified sobs and wails echoed through the classroom. There were even students in nearby rooms crying. The teacher quickly raised his voice. "I want you to know that she is alive. The doctors were able to restart her heart and they are keeping her under observation. The school will keep you informed."

Takeshi did his best to console Chiharu, but even he couldn't stop his body shaking. Naoko wept into her hands uncontrollably. She glanced over at the two empty desks and stammered, "Tomoyo must be a wreck."

School proceeded slowly and solemnly for the rest of

the week.

* * *

At the hospital, Franklin, Touya, and Yukito maintained vigil by Sakura's bedside, and hardly slept for days. Seconds drew out into eons, punctuated by dull beeps of the heart monitor. Franklin did not move from the bed, his hand firmly gripping his daughter's. Beside him, Touya and Yukito sat trembling.

A time came where Touya reached out, grabbed Yukito's hand, and gripped it tightly. As Yukito sat there, his fingers threaded through Touya's, his mind raced with fear and guilt. He could not shake images of the last time he'd seen Sakura, laying her very soul bare to him.

And I crushed her, he thought.

You did what you thought was right, said Yue, his voice betraying not an ounce of his own grief. *You cannot do more.*

Yes I can, Yukito's mind roared.

He stood and walked to the foot of Sakura's hospital bed. His body was shaking, as if he were about to confess murder. As he steeled himself, the door opened to admit Tomoyo and her mother, Sonomi. They both looked concerned – especially Tomoyo, whose eyes were blood red. Yukito almost backed out of his confession, but decided it was for the best.

"Mister Kinomoto," he said. Franklin looked up at him. "I am responsible for this."

"Yuki, don't be stupid," growled Touya.

"What do you mean, Mister Tsukishiro?" asked Franklin.

"Yesterday, Sakura came to my house, and confessed to me her wish to be my wife," Yukito explained. Tomoyo gasped, while Franklin let out an amused sigh.

"You turned her down," the father concluded.

"I am ashamed that I do not feel for her as she does for me," said Yukito. "I did not want to distract her from finding someone who would make her more happy than I could. She was clearly heart-broken. It is because of me that she collapsed. It is my fault that she is here now." He bowed reverently to Franklin. "If you would see me cast from your family, I will accept it."

Franklin stood up from the bed and walked to the boy. He looked into Yukito's face, and then he embraced the boy.

"I will not exile you for something so trivial," said Franklin, pulling away. "Sakura has been tired for months. Schoolwork, her movies, gymnastics, and let's not forget her kung-fu lessons on Saturdays. She burnt herself out." He coughed and held back his own tears. "It is my fault," he said. "I pressured her to study hard, and I failed to see her fatigue. It is sfault."

"Mine too," said Tomoyo. "I should have seen it too. But I overworked her." Sonomi pulled her into an embrace as she broke down.

Outside the hospital room, Xiaolang waited. He couldn't bring himself to go in and visit, despite Tomoyo's assurances he'd be welcome. In his hands, he held a bag in which Kero hid. The living teddy bear looked up at him and said, "I failed her too."

"To me, it sounds like you had no say in the matter," replied Xiaolang. "She overwhelmed you."

"She used the resonance link against me," replied Kero, shuddering at the thought. "A magician with half the skill of Clow couldn't do that, and she did it without breaking a sweat."

"It's a good thing, when you think about it," said Xiaolang with a shaky voice. "If she could do that, and transform seven Clow Cards in one go, then it means she's getting more powerful, right?"

Kero huffed. He reluctantly pondered the nature of Sakura's attack. When she pierced his mind to extract the answers she wanted, Kero could feel the grief fuelling her.

Her joy makes her powerful, but so does her wrath, he thought. *Not a good combination, I'd say. Maybe Yue was right all along,*

Clow.

Kero looked up at the boy and said, "We'll wait until she wakes up."

* * *

In the early hours of Friday morning, Sakura sat up. She gave a great big yawn, and looked around. Her mind drew a complete blank. She couldn't see very well, but the familiar beeping of a heart monitor told her she was in a hospital.

Then she recalled her last memory.

I must have changed all the Cards, she thought. *That'd've knocked me out cold.*

She jumped slightly at the sound of a gasp to her right. There sat her father, gripping her hand tightly. Heavy bags weighed down his eyes, which were red with worry. He sat beside her on the bed, held her tightly, and wept tears of joy. His sobs woke Touya and Yukito, who crept over to see the patient awake. Touya scrambled to the other side of the bed and threw his arms around his sister, and cried just as hard as his father.

Sakura just smiled amid them.

Yukito turned the lights on to their lowest level, such that Sakura could see his face. She looked at him hesitantly, and Yukito glanced right back at her. Then she offered her hand, and pulled him into their group hug.

Naturally, Sakura's classmates were delighted to hear she was awake. Tomoyo excitedly bought a big get-well Card for everyone in the class, including Eriol and Xiaolang, to sign. Then she, Chiharu, Takeshi, Xiaolang, and Naoko went to visit her in the hospital. Eriol tagged along as a chaperone.

Sakura beamed with joy at the sight of her friends, and at the Card signed by her whole class. Though there was one visitor, pretending to be a plush-toy on Tomoyo's shoulder, who dampened her spirits significantly. She couldn't speak to him without freaking the others out, so she reached out with her mind.

Kero shuddered at the sensation of her resonance, but remained still. Sakura gently tapped on the door to his mind, and he answered hesitantly.

I see you're awake, he said through their link.

Sakura couldn't reply at first, she was so ashamed of her actions.

I should not have lost it, she said. *I violated you, and forced you to tell me something you—*

I shoulda told ya, said Kero. *I shouldn't've said ya had all the time. An' I shouldn't've been playin' all them games when ya needed me. I'm sorry.*

I'm sorry too, replied Sakura.

Tears wet her face as she broke the link. Everyone else thought she was just touched by the Card and everyone's concern. That was how she wanted to keep it.

The group chatted for a while about Sakura's condition, and then talked about what had been happening at school. Takeshi told a tall tale about the source of the word 'coma,' for which Chiharu, unusually, *didn't* punish him. Eriol brought Sakura up to speed on their homework for the week, which made the poor girl cringe.

One by one, the visitors excused themselves, until only Xiaolang, Kero, and Tomoyo remained. Kero came to life and finally hugged his Master.

Then Xiaolang bowed and said, "I'm sorry for not telling you about the nature of the Cards sooner."

Sakura shook her head. "It's alright. You were looking out for me."

Then, Tomoyo sat down on the bed and looked fixedly at Sakura, who moved to hug her friend. Tomoyo furiously slapped Sakura across the face, her hand impacting with a loud crack that frightened Kero and Xiaolang. Sakura glared back at her friend, horrified and panicked. Tomoyo's face was a mix of rage and fear the likes of which Sakura had never seen.

Tomoyo fell against her, buried her face in the crook of

her neck, and gripped her friend. And she cried.

"My Sakura almost died," she wailed. "How dare you do that to me?! You horrible person!"

The left half of Sakura's face was numb, but the other half cringed as she put her arms around Tomoyo.

"I'm sorry," she said, gently stroking her hair.

* * *

It was another day before Franklin was allowed to take Sakura home. The doctor gave her a clean bill of health, but asked her to rest a few more days. That was quite the bother for Sakura, who didn't want to miss any more school and incur even more homework.

Sakura, Touya, and Franklin sat around the dinner table, feasting on a helping of Karaage á la Kinomoto. When they finished the plate of delicious fried chicken, Franklin announced, "I've been thinking."

"A dangerous pastime, Dad," said Touya.

"Oh, very dangerous," jibed Sakura.

Franklin chuckled, "Ah, yes. But I've been thinking of a vacation. You both have been very busy and overworked the last few weeks. Plus, we didn't go anywhere over the summer. Since Sakura's been asked to take some more days off, why don't we take a trip into the country?"

"Good idea," said Sakura.

"There's a house at Lake Inawashiro," said Franklin. "We can rent that for three days, and just relax. How does that sound?"

"That sounds great!" exclaimed Sakura, and went up-stairs to start packing. Touya glared suspiciously at Franklin.

"Inawashiro? Seriously?" he muttered.

"She's never met him," said Franklin. With a melancholic smile, he added, "Plus, *he* asked."

12 | Metanoia

Sakura heard a whirr of motors. Sunlight and wind buffeted her face. She opened her eyes and rubbed the sleep dust away. She looked up and noticed the car roof retracting into the trunk behind her. She looked straight ahead, and saw Touya's face.

"Oi, Kaiju!" he yelled over the wind. He then pointed to the right side of the car. Sakura saw a swath of smooth land that looked as if it were paved with a single mirror. Lake Inawashiro was absolutely beautiful, seemingly a portal to an upside-down world that was just as vibrant and breathtaking. On the other side of the lake, Sakura could see mountains stretching along the horizon, crowned by fluffy white clouds and endless blue skies.

With a wide smile, Sakura stretched and savoured the feeling of the wind in her hair.

"We're almost there," said Franklin. "Maybe another half an hour."

Sakura laid back and enjoyed the scenery all the way to the lodge. It was a modest house, but a bit bigger than their house in Tokyo. The two-storey building had a pleasant-blue coloured roof that stood out from the sky above. The inside smelled lived-in, but in a nice way. It felt like a loving family had lived there.

Sakura grabbed her bag and claimed one of the upstairs bedrooms for herself. She tested the bed, placed her bag in the closet, and then opened the window. She gazed out over the shore of Lake Inawashiro, breathing deep of its air. She didn't know why, but for some reason the place felt as if it were already a second home for her.

Well, I should go for a walk to get to know the place, she thought.

She trotted down stairs. Franklin was already on the way out to get groceries. Touya had found a nice spot on the couch and dozed.

"I was thinking of going for a walk," said Sakura.

His eyes still closed, Touya snickered, "Oh, no, the Kaiju will rampage all around–"

Sakura threw a couch cushion at him, but it didn't rub the smirk off his face.

"Where were you thinking of going?" asked Franklin. "If you're interested, there's a big mansion just up the hill. It has a really nice front garden."

Her interest piqued, Sakura set off. The mansion was quite a ways up the hill, but a combination of Xiaolang's training and Sakura's general fitness made the walk cinch.

Franklin wasn't joking. The mansion was huge; almost double the size of Tomoyo's place. It looked well cleaned and cared for, with white walls and maroon roof tiles. A vast garden surrounded the building, like a moat of green pockmarked with the most beautiful flowers.

Oh, my God! It's beautiful, she thought. She skirted around the outer walls of the mansion, trying her best to count the different flowers. The breeze blew gently and carried pollen to her nose. She breathed deep of their perfumes and sighed with contentment.

I can't remember the last time I wished to live in a place like this, she thought.

Sakura watched a little longer. Just as she moved to leave, a head poked up from beneath a hydrangea bush. It was an elderly man in gardening clothes and a broad-brimmed straw hat. He still had significant colour to his beard, which contorted as he smiled.

"Good day, Miss," he said. "I don't recognise your face."

Sakura smiled. "Oh, I just came from the house just down the hill," she explained.

"Ah, a new resident?" said the man with piqued interest.

"Not permanent," said Sakura. "We're just renting it for a few days." She bowed politely. "My name is Sakura Kinomoto."

"Masaki Amamiya," said the man with a bow. "Nice to meet you."

"Sorry to have disturbed you while you're gardening," said Sakura. "I just thought the house looked nice. And the garden is particularly beautiful."

"Well, thank you very much, Miss Kinomoto," said Masaki. "And you haven't disturbed me at all. In fact, I was almost finished weeding, and was thinking of having some tea. Would you care for some?"

He had such a nice demeanour that Sakura couldn't refuse. Nor could she resist the view of the lake the man's house afforded. She went around to the front gate of the mansion, taking note of the missing family nameplate that typically adorns such gates.

"Oh, never mind that," said Masaki. "It got a little rusty and I sent off for a new nameplate. Come on."

Sakura followed Masaki to the front door, adjacent to which a fresh pot of tea and two place settings had been laid on a table.

"Were you expecting guests already?" asked Sakura.

"My staff must have noticed you and put out another place setting," said the old man. He held out a chair for her, as a good gentleman does, and she served herself a scone and some tea. She took a sip, and then surveyed the house. It was indeed huge, but she could hear nothing from inside. It seemed the man lived alone.

"Oh, yes, besides my servants, it's just me," said Masaki.

"Don't you have family?" asked Sakura, a tad disappointed.

"I did," said Masaki, his beard crinkling as he smiled. "I had a dear daughter, and she would often play in this house. This very garden was one she planted herself. We worked on it together for many years."

"Where is she now, if I may ask?" asked Sakura.

Masaki just smiled, though there was sadness in his eyes as he looked upward.

"She was sick, you see," he said solemnly. "And, unfortunately, the doctors could do little for her."

Sakura's heart skipped a beat.

For the love of God, not again!

"I'm sorry I brought it up," she stammered.

"Never mind, dear," said Masaki, lifting her chin with a finger. "Pretty girls like you should smile." Sakura pushed aside her sadness and willed a smile. That made Masaki smile in return. "That's much better," he chirped. "Have some of the blueberry jam. My servants are excellent cooks."

Sakura tried some jam on her scone and it was simply delicious. It brought a real smile to her face and she immediately requested the recipe. Masaki proceeded to ask her about her family.

"There's my Big Brother, Touya," she explained. "And my Dad, Franklin."

"Franklin? Is he American?" asked Masaki. There was a slight catch to his voice that Sakura assumed was surprise.

"He's British," said Sakura. "My Msother was Japanese. She, umm ... She got sick too, a long time ago, and went ... up there." She pointed to the sky.

"As Britain's neighbours would say, *c'est la vie*," said Masaki.

"But I'm not lonely," said Sakura. "I have Dad and Big Brother, plus my best friend Tomoyo, and all my friends at school too. And we're all really happy. Except when my Big Brother is a meanie and likes to call me 'Kaiju.'"

Masaki chuckled.

"Such are boys. But it's good that you have such a close family," he said. He noted the Star Key hanging around her neck and said, "That's quite a beautiful necklace you have there, Miss Kinomoto." Sakura's hand drifted upward protectively. Masaki quickly stammered, "Apologies, I didn't mean to be rude."

Sakura chuckled, "No, no, it's just … This is a really important thing for me." She removed it and held it out to him. He studied it as a geologist would a specimen of fine diamond.

"This is a true treasure, Miss Kinomoto," said Masaki. "Look after it."

Sakura beamed, knowing the value of the necklace far more than the old man.

Masaki took another sip of tea and moved onto another subject. "Come to think of it, it is still in the middle of the school term. Unusual to take a family trip at such a time, wouldn't you say?"

Sakura sighed as she considered her experience a week ago.

"We're taking a vacation for my sake," she said. "I … umm … I've been working myself really hard at school and on projects and … I fainted last week. The doctors said I should take a vacation. So my father organised this trip."

Masaki pursed his lips and nodded slowly.

"He seems to be a good father," he intoned.

They finished tea. Sakura decided to go and finish her walk. Masaki showed her to the front gate. There, he said, "Miss Kinomoto, if you don't have plans, you would be more than welcome to come tomorrow. I don't entertain very much, you see, and it would be nice to have some company."

Sakura gazed at the old man, and could sense the loneliness in his eyes. It made her ache as much as his invitation elated her.

"Of course, Mister Amamiya," she said. She then bowed. "Thank you for the tea. See you tomorrow."

She trotted off down the hill back to the house. Evidently, Franklin hadn't returned, and Touya was still out like a light on the couch. Sakura gazed through the window and pursed her lips with residual guilt. She wondered how many times he'd watched her do magic without her knowledge, which he couldn't now.

No sense going down that path, now, she thought. *Get your strength back, okay?*

Sakura went back to walking, this time along the lakefront. She found a point along the road where she could get down to the shore, and took her shoes off. She felt the bite of the cold water, and the grainy goo of the silt sliding through her toes. Her eyes closed, she let the breeze flow through the strands of her hair.

Through the aether, she could sense the fish in the lake, the birds in the sky above, the clouds gathering on the horizon, the people going about their lives in the town up north. Amid that cacophony of sensations, she did not sense the joy and grief emanating from a pair of eyes fixated upon her.

* * *

The next day, Sakura showed up at Masaki's mansion. In her hand was a bag of homemade cookies Franklin had asked her to take.

"They're to say thanks for being nice to my favourite gal," her father had said.

Sakura met Masaki at the front gate. This time, he was dressed in a long sleeved shirt and a fine vest-trouser combination. Sakura almost didn't recognise the man in such formal attire.

"Maybe I should have dressed nicer," she mumbled gauchely as she eyed her cheap-looking green tee and jeans.

"Not at all, Miss Kinomoto," he said. "Please come in."

Sakura entered the house this time. She had a *Doctor Who* moment as she marvelled, "It looks even bigger inside."

Masaki led her through the various rooms of the mansion, some of which reminded her of *Beauty and the Beast*. When she said as much, Masaki asked, "Ah, so you're a fan of that film?"

Sakura thought a moment. "The animated one, yes. The live-action was … okay … *ish?*"

Masaki chucked as they reached the study. There were a number of pictures lining the wall, much of them including Masaki with various famous people. There was one of him with Ronald Reagan, another with Emperor Hirohito, and even one with Akihito.

"Ah, I ran quite a few important businesses in Japan over the years," Masaki explained. He pointed to one in which he was playing an old game with Shigeru Miyamoto. "See this one? I was asked to offer some marketing insight for the development of the first *Legend of Zelda* game."

"Kero's favourite game," mumbled Sakura.

"I beg your pardon?" asked Masaki.

"One of my friends just loves Zelda," said Sakura nonchalantly. She scanned the photos a little longer. Her heart jumped into her throat when she saw a recent photo of Masaki, shaking hands with Donald Trump.

"Ha, that man was *quite* the character, to say the least," said Masaki.

"You've had quite a life, Mister Amamiya," Sakura exclaimed. "To think, the only other place I've been outside Japan is Surrey in England."

"What kind of place is that?" asked Masaki.

"It was nice, but I haven't been back since Mum went away, so I don't remember much," said Sakura. "I should go back sometime."

Masaki invited her to the dining room, where a modest lunch had been set out. At Masaki's encouragement, Sakura helped herself to a plate of ham, salami, and pickled vegetables. As they ate, he asked her more questions about her friends and school life. She talked about the videos she and Tomoyo made, and even showed him one on her phone. Needless to say, he was impressed by the quality of the special effects and Sakura's acting (even though it wasn't acting).

"You're very artistic, Miss Kinomoto," said Masaki. "You remind me of my daughter." He pointed to a framed picture on the wall. The frame's glass protected the paper from the air, preserving the vibrant crayon drawing of a rainbow. Beneath the arc of colours, Sakura noticed two stick-figures holding hands.

"Is that you and your daughter?" asked Sakura.

"Indeed," said Masaki. "From the front balcony, you can see the most wonderful rainbows stretching over the lake. Rainbows were my daughter's favourite things."

Sakura gazed at the man, who still had a wide smile on his face. But his eyes told her that smile was forced with all his strength. She reached out and gripped his hand.

"You miss her, don't you?" she said.

"Very much," stammered the old man.

"It's a shame that she got sick," said Sakura. "I would have loved to meet her."

"She'd have adored you," said Masaki. "But rarely does life go the way you want. And often, you have to accept it, no matter how badly you want to control things. I learned that, if you try to control certain things, you end up spoiling them."

Sakura paused a moment, and considered her experience. She remained pensive, until Masaki broke her out of her reverie. "A penny for your thoughts?"

"I was just thinking about what you said," said Sakura. "There was a boy … *is* a boy. I loved him. And I coughed up the courage to tell him how I felt. But …" The thought still pained her.

"He turned you down?" asked Masaki.

Sakura nodded. "He wasn't mean. He was really polite,

and explained that he couldn't return my feelings. And ... I *still* feel. He's still part of my family – he's my older brother's best friend, you see."

"You'll probably always feel," said Masaki. "At least, a little bit. It's like grief." Sakura cringed at that, but remained silent. "Nevertheless, it doesn't mean you won't find someone else you love. And a sweet, kind girl like you will always find someone."

Sakura gave a hampered smile.

"I have gotten better, though," she said. "I feel happy but ... the world feels different. I feel different ... at least a little."

Masaki sipped his tea pensively. Then he looked at her with a straightforward gaze.

"Are you familiar with the works of Carl Jung?" he asked.

"Never heard of him," said Sakura.

"He was actually a world-famous psychologist," chuckled Masaki. "He said that when a person receives a tremendous shock, their soul would melt down and be reborn. He called it 'Metanoia.' Perhaps that is what you feel now. You felt so strongly for this boy that his rejection caused your mind and soul to transform. And now you see the world in a different light."

"That doesn't sound good," said Sakura as she cringed.

"Ah, but it means you're more adaptable now," said Masaki. "In the future, if you experience such pain again, you will be able to persevere, and take whatever life throws at you. Perhaps, your new look on the world will lead you to the real love of your life."

Sakura beamed at the thought.

Metanoia, huh?

She and Masaki finished lunch, after which the old man said, "There's something I'd like you to have."

He led her into a bedroom. From the closet, he procured a chest and presented it to her. Inside was a beige blouse and long red skirt. Masaki encouraged her to put in on, and gave her the room while she got dressed. When he saw her wearing the clothes, he finally, actually smiled.

"You look almost exactly like her," he said. "These clothes belonged to my daughter."

Sakura shuffled gauchely. "I don't know if I could take these, if they belonged to her."

"I'm sure she would have wanted them to go to a wonderful girl, such as yourself," said Masaki. "It would honour me if you kept them."

Sakura looked at herself in the mirror, and shuddered with warmth at the sight.

"Thank you," she said.

The time came for her to return to the summerhouse. And yet, she couldn't shake the need to give Masaki something in return. Even though he insisted that her smile was enough, Sakura couldn't stand for it.

As she mulled it over at the front door, the pouch of Cards hidden under her new dress hummed. Aqua reached out through the resonance link and said, "Think of the picture, Master. You can give him something no one else can."

Sakura caught his meaning and looked up at Masaki.

"I know something I can do for you, Mister Amamiya," said Sakura. "In about … ten minutes? Yes, ten minutes! I want you to go to your second floor balcony and wait there. Can you do that?"

Masaki frowned. "I suppose that's fine. But why?"

"Trust me on this," said Sakura. She then raced down the path to the front gate. She stopped, turned, and said, "And Mister Amamiya, don't worry about your daughter. My Mum was so happy with my Dad, and so she's in a good place now. Since your daughter was so happy with you, I just know she's in a wonderful place too. And my Mum will look after her." With a chipper smile, the girl turned and darted off down the road.

Masaki closed the door. His face remained stern, but the tears flowed all the same. He went to the second floor balcony just like he was asked. Two men and two women waited for him there. To the lady and her daughter, he said, "Thank you for preparing the meals, Missus Daidouji. And you as well, Miss Daidouji."

Sonomi and Tomoyo smiled. They then breathed a long sigh of relief, knowing that the sneaking around was over.

"It was fun, playing spy," said Tomoyo.

Masaki bowed to the ladies reverently. Then he turned to the shorter man and shook his hand.

"Touya, it's been far too long," said Masaki.

"Of course, Grandfather," said Touya.

"You still delight in teasing your sister, I hear," said Masaki sternly. "Careful, for you reap what you sow."

"Sakura makes it hard to resist," jibed Touya, earning him a chuckle from Masaki.

Then he turned to Franklin. The Englishman still inspired some ire, despite the years between their meetings.

"Your daughter has become a wonderful person, Franklin," he said sternly. "Thank you for allowing me to meet her."

"She's your granddaughter as well," said Franklin. "I had hoped the meeting would have been sooner."

Masaki trembled and said, "When you informed me about her accident, I remembered Nadeshiko's sickness. I feared that Sakura might have veered down that path. Although it was just fatigue, I realised I had to meet her." Masaki walked to the balcony and looked out over the lake. He drew a deep breath and finally said, "I am sorry for not acknowledging your marriage to my daughter."

Franklin wet his lips and said, "I wasn't exactly a good suitor. I was a washed-up man, lost in the world, before I met Nadeshiko. I grabbed onto the thing that made me happy, and I didn't consider your feelings."

"No," sobbed Masaki. "I was just being stubborn. I should have just accepted that this was the path Nadeshiko would take. Had I done that, I'd not have ruined my bond with her and—" He braced himself against the railing of the balcony and buried his face in his hand. His body shook with every cough, hiccough, and tearful wail he repressed.

It took a moment before he realised something was in his hand. He wiped his free-falling tears aside and held up the nadeshiko flowers that had appeared in his hand.

"What?" he stammered. Franklin and Sonomi also appeared confused, but Touya and Tomoyo exchanged knowing glances.

"Mister Kinomoto, look!" said Tomoyo, pointing to the sky.

Masaki looked up and his jaw dropped in joyful awe. The brightest rainbow he'd ever seen crowned the lake. He could see every colour mirrored in the drawing Nadeshiko had made as a child. In that instant, he could almost see his beloved daughter seated on the balcony with him, sketching that rainbow.

"How?" he exclaimed. "It hasn't rained today … how did she know?"

"Sakura's a girl who makes things happen," said Touya. When Masaki and Franklin looked at him with equally befuddled looks, he added, "Trust me on this, Grandfather. She really is magical."

Neither Masaki nor Franklin caught his true meaning, but they smiled nonetheless. They gazed at the rainbow, and thought proudly of the little girl who heralded it.

* * *

Sakura rode in the front seat on the way home. Thanks to that, she got control of the radio, and had paired her phone to play her music. She started dancing, while Touya watched and tried not to laugh.

"So, you both had a good time?" asked Franklin.

"Nice and chillaxed," said Touya.

"And Mister Amamiya was so nice!" exclaimed Sakura. "I can't wait for the next school event when I can wear that dress."

"Ain't it a little old fashioned?" asked Touya. Sakura just poked her tongue at him.

"And thank you, Dad, for setting this up," she said.

"You're most welcome!" said Franklin.

Sakura added, "And you know what, I'm gonna play your favourite song." She searched for the file on her phone, and hit play. Franklin and Touya laughed at the voice of The Proclaimers blaring through the speakers.

And together, they sang along to 'I'm gonna be.'

13 | Return to Joy

A warm welcome awaited Sakura at school. Everyone was so excited to see her again, even people she'd had little contact with during her school years. Most greetings came with a request for more Cardcaptor videos. Sakura was glad for all the support, and thanked everyone who greeted her in the halls.

Of course, she cringed at the amount of homework awaiting her. Tomoyo helped her study, but on the days where she had chorus club, Xiaolang took over. In three days, Sakura was all caught-up on schoolwork, and her mood was still bright as it had ever been.

"Well done," said Franklin when she came home with the announcement. "I think that deserves a bit of a celebration." He finished stirring the soup on the stove and handed her a flier he'd found earlier that day. The ad read, 'Tsukimine Shrine, Reopening Festival.'

"They repaired the damage done by that crazy girl with the bombs," explained Franklin. "I'm sure you'd love to go for some takoyaki?"

Sakura's mouth watered at the mention of her favourite snack food. Then, of course, there was taiyaki, and okonomiyaki. Not to mention, Kero was bound to psychically pester and cajole her until she supplied him with his beloved Modern-Yaki.

She checked the date.

"It's tomorrow night," said Sakura. "I wonder if people will have time."

"Of course, they will," said Franklin. "Tomorrow's Friday, after all."

The next day was far more lax than the previous few days had been, now that all the homework was out of the way. Sakura and her friends decided to eat lunch in the schoolyard. As they ate, she suggested they all attend the festival – a suggestion well received.

"I'd love to go," exclaimed Tomoyo. Her expression suddenly went glum. "But it's Mother-Daughter day today. I already arranged to have dinner with Mom."

"You should spend time with her," said Sakura with a smile.

"I'm sorry, but I have a screen writing class tonight," said Naoko, her eyes drooping with disappointment.

"Oh, so you're going to learn how to write movies?" asked Sakura. "I can't wait to see something you've written, Naoko." The bespectacled girl grinned in response.

"Takeshi and I'd like to go, but we've got our three year anniversary this afternoon," said Chiharu. She glanced at Takeshi with a gauche but excited gleam to her eyes. Sakura wondered whether Chiharu was expecting a marriage proposal.

"Yep, it's our anniversary, which I've been planning for a while," said Takeshi with a warm smile directed at his girlfriend. "So we won't be able to make it to the festival."

"So it's just me then," said Sakura. She felt a twinge of disappointment, but was glad that her friends were pursuing their dreams.

"Speaking of festivals," blurted Takeshi. "We call them *matsuri*, but do you know why? It's because people used to wait – *matsu* – a long time to get to the shrine. And lines used to get as long as one league – *ri* – and the people would get bored. So, the government set up stalls along the line so people wouldn't get bored."

"Really?" exclaimed Sakura. Even Naoko and Tomoyo looked a little convinced.

Chiharu glared at her boyfriend, but bore a conflicted look in her eyes. Takeshi looked at her, a wide grin on his face as if to challenge, *Go on, tell me I'm fibbing*. But she just couldn't.

"That might be right," she mumbled.

"Haha! Victory!" exclaimed Takeshi. He shocked Chiharu a little, who then started to laugh.

"I wish you didn't have to go alone," said Tomoyo to Sakura. "Why not invite Mister Lee? He's helped you out with your homework too. Not to mention the combat lessons."

Sakura pondered a moment, and realised her friend had a point. She glanced around the schoolyard, but couldn't see the Chinese boy.

"That's weird, he usually eats with us," said Naoko.

Takeshi interjected, "I think I saw him playing basketball with his classmates. Mister Lamperouge is there with them."

For some reason Sakura couldn't comprehend, she really wanted to watch the game. She quickly finished her lunch and excused herself. Tomoyo followed her with a DSLR in-hand, ready to capture the emotions Sakura was sure to express. They found the basketball courts, where a group of school students had gathered to spectate the game.

Sakura had expected to see a team of boys playing on the asphalt, but there were only two. The rest of the team had moved to the sidelines. Xiaolang faced off against the slightly taller Eriol. The substitute teacher had the ball, which he deftly dribbled as he grinned. Sakura pushed through the crowd to the wire fence and yelled in support for the pair.

Eriol glanced over and waved ecstatically, while Xiaolang just looked befuddled. Then, the Scotsman shot him a grin made his blood boil. Eriol passed him the ball and assumed a defensive stance. Xiaolang started dribbling and advanced slowly, his eyes on the teacher. Then he advanced to the right, but feinted and went left. He tried to dart past Eriol and took a shot at the ring. Eriol swiped in mid-air and intercepted the ball. He withdrew to the centre line and came back against the livid Chinese boy. He double-feinted and Xiaolang tripped, giving him enough time to take a shot.

Nothing but net.

"Careful, or ya might get grannied," chuckled Eriol amid the cheers of the crowd.

Xiaolang scrambled to his feet and grabbed the ball. He stomped back to the centreline and tried again. He tried to spin around Eriol, who fell for his feint. He raced to the basket and leapt up to slam-dunk it.

"No chance of that now, is there?" said Xiaolang with a very bad imitation of a Scottish accent. He tossed a grinning Eriol the ball and snarled, "Now, haud yer wheesht, Scottie. Let's play!"

Eriol looked really serious now. His speed tripled, so much that Xiaolang couldn't see him. He'd darted around the boy and threaded the ball in an instant. Then he held his hands out in a gloating gesture.

"Dude, that is like, my mad skill!" he bellowed in a terrible American accent.

The gloves are off now, thought Xiaolang. He reached deep within and seized the power of his wing-chun reflexes. Dribbling the ball, he advanced. He moved with incredible speed, but changed direction faster than Eriol could see. He spun and darted, zigzagging his way toward the basket, tiring his opponent out in the process. Then he made the leap toward the basket.

Within the depths of his mind, he detected something. A voice spoke to him through the aether, in a manner not unlike a resonance link. The voice said to him, "*Fàngsōng.*

Guānzhù nǐ de mùbiāo."[7]

His competitive mindset gone, Xiaolang took a deep breath, and then flicked his wrist. The ball left his hand, and sailed through the net.

Time resumed and everyone cheered his score. But he was completely befuddled, as if he'd forgotten where he was. He looked over at Eriol, who still had that same insufferable grin. He clapped for the boy just as the bell rang. As the spectators dispersed and headed back to class, Eriol marched past the boy and whispered in fluent Mandarin, "If you remain calm and focus on your objective, you will become much stronger."

"Since when do you speak Mandarin, Lamperouge?" asked Xiaolang.

"A wizard did it," shrugged the man, and he went back to class.

The words echoed in Xiaolang's mind as he neared the edge of the basketball court, mesmerising and frustrating him. What did this insufferable man know? He was just good at playing basketball and making annoying wisecracks. What did he know about strength?

Xiaolang mulled and mulled and mulled. A tap on his shoulder broke him out of his ponderings. There was Sakura, smiling at him. He almost fainted in shock as blood filled his face.

"You played really well," said Sakura. Her perkiness immobilised him, and he couldn't think of a response. "What's the matter?" asked the girl.

"Nothing," he finally replied. Nearby, Tomoyo silently chuckled. Xiaolang shrugged her off and said, "We should probably get to class."

Sakura fell alongside him and walked with a skip in her step.

"I'd wanted to ask if you were doing anything tonight," said Sakura. "They've reopened Tsukimine Shrine after

---

7   Mandarin: "Relax. Focus on your objective."

Alice Axilotl. I was thinking of going. Would you like to come too?"

Xiaolang glanced at Tomoyo. "Daidouji is coming too?"

"Prior plans," replied Tomoyo with an evil chortle.

"Well, I'm sure Kerberus won't let you go alone," said Xiaolang.

"I'm not keen on dealing with him telepathically harassing me," replied Sakura with a cringe.

"So ... It'll just be the two of us," the boy stammered.

"Will that be a problem?" asked Sakura.

Xiaolang's heart skipped a beat and he blurted, "No, not at all. It'd be nice to go to the festival with you."

"Yay!" chirped Sakura. "Come around to my place at six. Okay?" She chuckled giddily and skipped off to class with Tomoyo in tow. As the paparazza passed him, she whispered, "Lee and Sakura, Sittin' in a Tree ..."

"Shut up," replied a blushing Xiaolang.

* * *

Xiaolang timidly approached the Kinomoto house. His body was shaking, but not due to the approaching cold of winter. In fact, he was quite hot in his jacket and scarf combo. He took them off as he ascended the steps to the front door. He took a few long breaths to steady himself.

Come on, you idiot, he thought. *I've spent time alone with her before. It's not like this is a date.*

He suddenly wondered whether this was a date. Before he could consider the possibility, however, his hand had already pushed the doorbell. Dread filled him, fuelled by the sound of approaching footsteps. He almost ran screaming.

The door opened, and there was Sakura in a yellow long-sleeve cardigan and jeans. She was positively stunning, and could not have been more beautiful if she wore a diamond-encrusted dress. Her smile widened excitedly as she beckoned him inside. He entered the house not for the first time, yet it still felt like alien territory.

Sakura led him into the dining room, where Touya sat and glared daggers at him.

"What're you doin' here, creep?" grumbled Touya.

"He and I are going to the Tsukimine Shrine," said Sakura disapprovingly. "I'd invite you, but not if you're gonna be like that."

Touya ignored her and stood over Xiaolang. The Chinese boy's nervousness subsided and he composed himself against his former opponent.

"Sakura tells me you understand English," he said with Sakura's English accent. "You be nice, ya hear? No tryin' to have it off with her, got it?"

Xiaolang inhaled sharply with embarrassment, while Sakura indignantly exclaimed, "Touya! That's disgusting!"

"Agreed," said another voice. Franklin entered the room and looked fixedly at his son. "It's good you're looking out for her, but keep a gentlemanly tongue. Understood?"

"Got it," said Touya. He grabbed his backpack and announced his departure to his part time job. He tussled Sakura's hair and chortled, "Have fun, Kaiju."

"Big Brother, you messed up my hair!" exclaimed the girl. She grabbed a mirror off the bench and groaned at her dishevelled appearance. Meanwhile, Franklin just stared at Xiaolang. When the man cleared his throat loud enough, Sakura snapped to attention and walked over. "Sorry," she said. "Xiaolang Lee, this is my father, Franklin. Dad, this is Xiaolang."

Franklin shook his hand firmly. "Nice to finally meet you, Mister Lee. I apologise for my son's rude words."

"Not at all, sir," stammered Xiaolang. "It's good that she has so many people looking out for her." Beside them, Sakura rolled her eyes and returned to fixing her hair.

"Sorry, Xiaolang, just give me a few minutes," she said. She went to her bedroom, grumbling about Touya, and left

Xiaolang alone with Franklin. The man sized him up, though he had an approving look on his face.

"I hear you'd been teaching Sakura self-defence," he said. "Given what happened at Tsukimine Shrine last time, I'd say it's a good idea."

"She asked," said Xiaolang curtly. "And I haven't pushed her or done anything dangerous."

*Now **that's** a load of crap,* he told himself.

"At ease, soldier," said Franklin facetiously. "You're the first boyfriend she's brought home, and you've already set the bar high."

"Boyfriend!" Xiaolang choked. He tried not to sound too hopeful as he asked, "Did *she* say that?"

"Nope, but trust me, a father knows things," said Franklin with a smile. He offered Xiaolang a cup of tea, which he accepted, and the pair sat at the table. The boy was still very nervous as he searched for something to discuss with the man. Some semblance of a topic came to mind and he opened his mouth.

"So ... Sakura told me you took on your wife's name," he stammered. "Is that common in Britain?"

Franklin shrugged, "Not really." He eyed the picture of his wife and added, "Nadeshiko and I actually decided over a game of rock-paper-scissors."

Xiaolang almost sprayed his tea. "Are you serious?"

"Dead serious, my friend," said Franklin. "Before, my surname was Avalon."

"Ah, as in King Arthur," chuckled Xiaolang. The name churned in his head, as he recalled books he'd read with his own father a long time ago. Visions of his father's library, fuelled by their common passion for archaeology, surged through his mind, before he finally remembered. "Wait a minute," he said, his finger raised fixedly. "You wouldn't by chance be *the* Doctor Franklin Avalon? Of the Cambridge Department of Archaology?"

Franklin chuckled. "Yep, that's me ... in another life, at least."

Xiaolang's eyes lit up with excitement.

"My father and I are huge fans of your work," he exclaimed. "We read all the books you'd written on the Nostratic Culture. It was so fascinating!"

Franklin waved him off gauchely. "You're one of the few who enjoyed it. Most others thought it was more Tolkienian than real history. One of my peers suggested I publish a mythopoetic fiction novel."

"They're wrong," said Xiaolang, his eyes wide with amazement. "My father thinks you might have been on to something. I remember your discussions on the Silver Key the Nostratics worshiped. Did you manage to find it?"

"Nope," said Franklin with a disappointed grimace. "I blew quite a bit of money looking for it too. Eventually, the faculty told me to drop it. Quite depressing, if you ask me. But, in hindsight, it's good that I failed. If I hadn't, I wouldn't have met Nadeshiko, and Sakura and Touya wouldn't be here." He regarded his wife's photo with a warm smile. "All in all, a win, I say."

Sakura appeared not long after to find Xiaolang and Franklin chatting amiably. The sight lifted her spirits even more. Xiaolang stood from the table and thanked his host for the tea. Then they went to the door. Franklin gave the customary warning to have his daughter back before ten, and then wished them a fun time.

The pair walked in silence a while. Sakura eventually spoke up and said, "I'm so glad you and Dad got along."

"Me too," said Xiaolang. "You should have told me he was an archaeologist. My father followed his work when he was at Cambridge."

"Really?" exclaimed Sakura. "Well, what a coincidence that we'd end up together."

Together, screeched his frazzled mind. With a rosy-cheeked grimace, he asked, "Did you tell your Dad this was a date?"

"No," said Sakura, perplexed. "I'd invited everyone else out, but they all had plans."

"Even Daidouji?" asked Xiaolang, wondering where the camera-obsessed girl was hiding.

"She said it was Mother-Daughter day," said Sakura. She pursed her lips and added, "I doubt that though. She's probably on a date with her girlfriend." Xiaolang gave her a confused glance. "She told me that she only likes girls."

"Ah, I see," said Xiaolang, diverting his eyes.

"You knew, didn't you?" asked Sakura.

"She told me, yeah," said Xiaolang. "I, umm ... I was surprised, really. I didn't picture her in that way."

Sakura decided to pry a little more. "When did she tell you?"

Oh, crap, I can't tell her I figured it out on my own.

"Oh, I, uh... I asked her out," Xiaolang finally blurted. "But she said she only likes girls."

Sakura just laughed in a manner that made Xiaolang want to kiss her right then and there.

"No wonder I thought you two were a couple," she said. "She kept looking at you a certain way, and I thought that was love. But, it's taught me that I need to pay more attention."

Then pay more attention to my face, Xiaolang growled behind his kind smile.

They reached Tsukimine Shrine, only to find it absolutely full of people. A perturbed Sakura approached one of the families waiting on the outskirts of the crowd, who explained that they'd been waiting to visit the shrine for almost an hour. Apparently, all the food stalls and games had sold out as well.

"Is this shrine that popular?" asked Xiaolang.

Sakura hung her head in disappointment. "They say a great sage built the shrine centuries ago. So lots of people come around." She checked her watch with a whine. "It's only quarter-past-seven!"

"Nothing we can do, though," said Xiaolang.

Sakura bowed to him. "Sorry for dragging you out."

"No, not at all," said Xiaolang. He had an idea.

"There's another place we can go. If you're interested, that is."

Sakura's eyebrows rose with piqued interest.

14 | Dancing High in the Sky

When one thinks nightclubs in Tokyo, it's usually *ageHa* with its gigantic dance floor, or *Feria* for those with the inclination for high class and style. But there is a far lesser known one, in the back alleys of Shinjuku, called *Tsubasa*.

"A nightclub?" murmured Sakura nervously as they stood in front of the building. "I'm only sixteen, so I can't go here. Plus, they're really rowdy."

"Not this place," said Xiaolang. "I know the manager, so they'll let us in, and they have mocktails too. We'll be alright."

"Are you sure?" asked Sakura, wringing her hands nervously.

"This is a really safe place, Sakura," he said. "I tell my classmates that this is a good place for a date."

Sakura smirked mischievously. "Oh, so this is a date, eh?"

"No, I didn't have that intention," stammered Xiaolang. "It's just a nice place, and I think you'll like it."

Sakura took another glance at the building and decided to give him the benefit of the doubt. She motioned for him to lead, and they entered the club. Contrary to what Sakura believed about rowdy nightclubs, this one was quite tame. It was well lit, and smelled slightly on the sweeter side of neutral. It was filled with people, tucked away into alcoves, chatting and laughing. A dance floor was moderately occupied by couples, slowly swaying to music from a band on a small stage.

"You're right, I do like it," said Sakura.

One of the waitresses led them to a vacant alcove, and gave them a menu. There was only finger food on the menu, and only on the first page. The remaining ten were drinks, and most of them seemed alcoholic. Xiaolang went ahead and ordered some takoyaki, knowing it was Sakura's favourite, while the girl scanned the drinks menu for something she could legally order.

"Oh, we can do anything without alcohol," said the waitress.

"Really? Then, I'll have a ... Cinderella, thank you," said Sakura. The waitress left, leaving Sakura to look across the table at Xiaolang. "This is really a nice place," she said with an excited smile. She shuddered giddily. "It actually feels like a date, though, doesn't it?"

"Well, we can say it's not a date if you like," stammered Xiaolang. "But, I don't want to ... since ... you know, after Tsukishiro and everything." Sakura chuckled as a slight cold snap pitter-pattered through her chest. Her lingering sadness tempered her smile, and Xiaolang could see it. "Sorry," he said. "I didn't mean to bring it up."

"No, not at all," said Sakura. "It's the elephant in the room, isn't it?" She looked downward with a sigh. "Yukitos's actually really wise. He must get it from Yue."

"How so?" asked Xiaolang.

"Well, he knew that my feelings for him were ..." she grimaced as she searched for the right words. She finally blurted, "It's like this: I hardly knew him. Sure, he was Touya's best friend. And I knew he ate a lot. But when I was looking for fimo to make the shisa, I didn't know what colours to pick. I didn't know what colours he liked. On the other hand, Chiharu! She knew exactly what to get Yamazaki. She knows his favourite food and colours, and knows about his interests. And she adores him, but you wouldn't know it by her flip-outs when he starts fibbing."

That made Xiaolang chuckle.

"I wonder whether he likes being strangled," he said.

"I know," exclaimed Sakura. "But, with Yukito, I don't really know much about him, except that he's Yue's disguise. Did you know he's a Christian?"

"That comes as a surprise," replied Xiaolang.

Sakura went on, "And I think I fell in love with him straight away, but I just idealised him. I created a perfect boyfriend in my head, and put his name and face to it. And because of that, I spent all my time trying to impress him. I didn't try to learn more about him. I don't think I was very fair. And he knew it."

Xiaolang stared back at her, his own heart aching that she would put herself down so. In that moment, he almost wanted to reach out and hold her hand, if only to comfort her a little. But before he could summon the courage, the waitress appeared with their food and drinks. Sakura's mood brightened at the sight of takoyaki, and she lanced one with a fork.

"Plus," she added with a mouthful of fried squid batter. "It doesn't really help that he's gay."

Xiaolang almost choked on his drink. Sakura giggled at the sight.

"Did he tell you that?" he spluttered.

"He said he likes Touya," replied Sakura with a shrug. "They make a nice couple." She swallowed another takoyaki. "It's one of the reasons I changed so many Cards at once. I felt terrible. I didn't notice that Yukito was disappearing because my powers weren't good enough. Touya ended up giving his power to Yukito, and he knew about me and the Cards all along. I'd not even considered Tomoyo's orientation, either. I started to wonder how she'd felt, going through that discovery all on her own. I felt like I'd failed them all."

She spoke so neutrally, it was as if she were talking about an ordinary day. But Xiaolang could sense that she was still upset by it. This time, he did reach out. He just touched her hand, rather than held it, and said, "You haven't failed anyone, Sakura. So what if you didn't notice Tsukishiro and your brother, or Daidouji? It's not like they have a big sign on their heads." He withdrew his hand nervously, but kept talking. "I need to confess, I'd known about the Cards as well. After you went to hospital the first time, I told Kerberus and Yue that we should tell you. But they were worried that you'd, you know, do exactly what you did, and get sick from it. I'm sorry I didn't tell you either. I didn't want you to hurt yourself."

Sakura beamed and grabbed his hand.

"Thank you," she said warmly.

"You're welcome," said Xiaolang. "I'm glad to be part of your support team."

"Me too," said Sakura as she gobbled another takoyaki. "And I suppose it's all been good, since it's taught me I need to pay more attention to the people in my life."

"How so?" asked Xiaolang.

"Be less focused on myself and find out about the people around me," said Sakura.

Xiaolang frowned. "I think you do that already. You play games with Kerberus, you bake with Daidouji, and you listen to Yamazaki's nonsense all the time. And by the way, you bought the Book of Clow as a present for Yanagisawa, because she liked fantasy and magical things. Seems to me like you pay a lot of attention." Sakura blushed. "Remember the training in Tokushima? You sat with me and asked me about my interests."

"I remember that," chuckled Sakura. "Oh, by the way, totally get where you were coming from with *Poltergeist*."

"Ugh, I still don't like seeing TV static," moaned Xiaolang.

Sakura leaned forward with a smile and asked, "What else then? What other movies?"

"I liked the *Ip Man* movies," said Xiaolang. "The ones with Donnie Yen."

"He's the blind guy in *Rogue One*, right?" asked Sakura. "He was hilarious."

"Ah, but my father doesn't like him," replied Xiaolang. "He trained under the real Ip Man, and he'd watch those movies and say, 'This is wrong. That never happened. These movies are terrible.'"

Sakura chortled, "Just like my Dad when we watched *Kingdom of Heaven*. He'd keep pointing out where it was wrong." Her cheerfulness goaded her to ask more questions. "What about music?"

"Well, mostly Chinese music," said Xiaolang. "Though, I like the classics like Mozart too."

"Any western music?" Sakura pressed.

"The Beatles were really good," said Xiaolang. "Though The Proclaimers are decent too."

"Dad loves them," exclaimed Sakura. "I like Queen and David Bowie."

"Let me guess, you sang 'Starman' when the Falcon Heavy went into space," jibed Xiaolang.

"What Ziggy fan wouldn't?" replied Sakura.

Now Xiaolang just had to ask, "Okay, since we're talking western music, and ... since you're a girl, I have to ask: Justin Bieber?"

"No," said Sakura flatly.

Xiaolang accepted the answer, then he slowly asked, "BTS?"

"God, no!" blurted Sakura, cringing at the thought.

Xiaolang clapped his hands together and praised the Heavens. "Thank you, God!" His reaction was so comical, Sakura almost sprayed her Cinderella mocktail out her nose. There was a bit of splatter from her mouth as she cough-laughed, which landed on Xiaolang's sleeve. Sakura apologetically – though still laughing – took a napkin to clean his sleeve.

When she pulled back his sleeve, she noticed something on his left forearms.

"What's this?" she asked.

Xiaolang hesitantly rolled back his sleeve to reveal a tattoo of a light blue horse with a rainbow mane. It was drawn in a cartoon style Sakura had seen on toy-store billboards all around the place.

"It's a tattoo of Rainbow Dash from *My Little Pony*," said Xiaolang, his tone of voice a little hampered. "A friend and I, back in California, were really into the show. So we got these tattoos."

"You liked the show that much that you got permanent tattoos?" asked Sakura.

"Don't worry," said Xiaolang. "I'm not a weirdo."

"No, it's not that," replied Sakura. "I just don't see the appeal of the show. I never thought it was that good."

Xiaolang scoffed facetiously and said, "Oh, Miss Kinomoto, you are clearly hammered." He took her empty glass and held it up to the waitress. "Another mocktail for the lady, please."

Sakura put her hands on her hips. "Trying to get me drunk, Mister Lee?"

"Oh, yes, of course!" replied Xiaolang pompously. "What better way than to feed you non-alcoholic drinks?"

The two of them burst into laughter. Their joking and antics earned them a few smiles from other patrons. They continued chatting about various interests and events as the band played. Eventually, three empty food plates and six glasses sat on the table. Sakura and Xiaolang had discussed a great deal of topics, and had reduced themselves to listening to the music.

The band finished an upbeat song, to a round of modest applause from the patrons. Then one of them put his electric guitar aside for a voilin, and the male backing vocals stepped forward to the lead position. A pleasant sound echoed from the violin as the vocalist began to sing a soft melody to the rhythm of the drums.

"I've never heard this song before," murmured Xiaolang, enthralled by the music. He turned to Sakura, who had a look of nostalgia.

"This is 'High' by Lighthouse Family," she said. "I haven't heard this since Kindergarten."

As the chorus rang, Sakura found the beat infecting her body, and she bobbed along with it. She glanced at Xiaolang, who was smiling at her. She couldn't help but recall his appearance in her classroom, two months ago, and his smile at her dancing. She felt overcome with the need to dance once more. She slipped out of the alcove and beckoned him to the dance floor. He took some coaxing, but he soon joined her. Together, they bobbed their bodies to the song.

Sakura's heart raced with merriment. In one moment, she was chuckling at the sound of the music. The next, she found herself staring into Xiaolang's eyes. With each glance his way, she found herself gravitating toward him, until she joined hands with him. He twirled her, before gently pulling her into his embrace. As he did, Sakura turned rigid with shyness, and her heart fluttered at their sudden closeness. She willed herself to look into his eyes, where she saw the same hesitation. He too trembled at their proximity, but the look in her eyes gave him courage.

Sakura heard no music in her head. She felt no need to fantasise or impress. There was nothing to offer or expect. It was just them, and the music they both heard.

Her courage grew, and she moved closer still to him. She rested her head against his shoulder, as if it were a completely natural and obvious thing to do. Together, they swayed to the music from the violin and the man's soothing voice, singing the promise of one day being together in the sky.

And everything was just nice.

15 | Battle above Chiba

Chip packets and drink bottles littered the bedroom floor, as they often did when Sakura and Tomoyo had their girl's nights. Despite the heavy consumption of junk food, it was quite easy to know how the girls kept their figures when one factored in the real glutton.

Kero had reduced himself to a ball rolling about on the floor, completely stuffed with food. He burped, gurgled, and chuckled with delight.

"That's a good feedin'!" he proclaimed.

"Thanks for blowing all my allowance," droned Sakura, though it was hardly a hefty price to see Kero make a complete fool of himself.

Other issues occupied Tomoyo's mind. "C'mon, Sakura. I came here to ask about your date with Lee last night."

Sakura waved her off, grimacing to hold back her embarrassed yet excited smile. She focused on Kero. "I've been meaning to ask, where does all that food go?"

"Einstein," blurted Kero as if it were obvious. He stroked his food belly and said, "All the food gets converted into energy, a hundred and ten per cent efficiency."

"Kero, I'm not that good at science and even I know that's nonsense," said Sakura flatly.

"Sakura!" cried Tomoyo. "I'm dying here. Details, I say! Details!"

"Yeah, tell us all about the Brat," growled Kero.

"He's not a brat," said Sakura firmly. She huffed and finally turned to Tomoyo. "Tsukimine Shrine was overcrowded so we went somewhere else. He took me to this club called Tsubasa."

"A nightclub!" snapped Kero. "What, he tried ta slip ya a roofie?"

"No, Kero," exclaimed Sakura.

"But a nightclub?" asked a worried Tomoyo.

"It wasn't one of those rowdy ones," said Sakura. "It was actually a really nice, quiet place. And all the drinks on the menu non-alcoholic. Really delicious. Plus, the takoyaki was really good. And they even had little mini okonomiyaki."

"Modern-Yaki!" screamed Kero. "Why didn't you take me? I wanna go! I wanna go!"

Sakura gave him a little flick to silence him.

"We'll go next weekend," she said.

"You'd better!" snapped Kero.

Tomoyo, her curiosity burning, tapped Sakura's shoulder desperately. "What about Lee?"

"He was a perfect gentleman," said Sakura with a warm smile. "He didn't try anything. He didn't even suggest it was a date."

"Oh, it so was a date!" exclaimed Tomoyo.

"We talked about Yukito and the Cards," Sakura went on. "Then we started talking about movies, and music. I found out he likes *My Little Pony*." Tomoyo's eyes widened suspiciously. "Oh, he assures me he's not weird. And then we … we just talked about so many different things. And he's so funny. And …" Her cheeks simmered with warmth and her breathing quickened.

Tomoyo's jaw widened in anticipation. "What?"

"We danced," Sakura stammered. "I'd never danced like that before. I'd never been held like that before." Her heart fluttered at the memory.

A stringent sound broke her out of her reverie. It started low and grew in volume. Sakura glanced at Tomoyo. The girl's cheeks were blood-red and her eyes loaded with joy. She suddenly exploded and started jumping up and down excitedly.

"That's awesome!" she screeched. Her eyes went skyward and she proclaimed, "I'm gonna have to make a wedding dress soon!"

"Tomoyo! Going a little fast, don't you think?" cried Sakura.

"But it's clear you've found someone!" cried Tomoyo. "You and Lee are so perfect."

The notion made Sakura feel uncomfortable. It felt wonderful to be with Xiaolang, but a wall in her mind kept her from the thought of being in love. Be it the pain of Yukito's rejection, or the silly feeling she got thinking of how she'd behaved around him, something made her hesitate.

Tomoyo sensed her conflict, and threaded her fingers into Sakura's hand.

"Sakura, you shouldn't overthink it," she said. "If he makes you happy, you should be with him."

"No, she shouldn't," growled Kero. He crossed his arms tightly over his chest and huffed. "He's not right for you, Sakura. He's just a Brat."

"Kero, you hardly know him," said Sakura. "You shouldn't judge him just because he made a bad impression the first time."

"Pah, once a Brat, always a Brat," retorted Kero.

"*I* think you should be his girlfriend," Tomoyo stated. "You're wonderful together. I can see it in your face."

Sakura, wishing to be done with the subject, switched the focus to Tomoyo.

"And what about you, Miss Daidouji?" she said. "When am I gonna meet this older girlfriend of yours?"

Tomoyo withdrew and coughed.

"I don't know," she stammered. "I'm not sure you'd like her."

Sakura took Tomoyo's hand and said, "Trust me, if she's your girlfriend, I'll like her."

Tomoyo shuffled and averted her gaze. She swallowed as her eyes shifted nervously. She finally stammered, "I … She … my girlfriend … she hasn't told her parents. So I … I just don't want to do things prematurely, in case it gets out." She finally met Sakura's gaze and said, "Let me think about it, okay?"

Sakura stroked her friend's cheek and said, "Okay."

Kero floated over and landed on Tomoyo's head. He gave her forehead a comforting pat. Then he looked down at her and asked, "Ya told ya Ma, right?"

"Last night," said Tomoyo with a smile. "Telling Sakura gave me strength, and so I did it over Mother-Daughter night. And she told me she couldn't wait until I brought a nice girl home to meet her."

"That's wonderful," said Sakura. "It'll be so good to meet her too. We'll all have to go to Tsubasa together."

"Don't forget me!" bellowed Kero.

Before Sakura could chide her glutinous guardian, a familiar sensation burst through her mind like nothing she'd felt before. Both she and Kero glanced at the window and high into the early afternoon sky.

"Clow!" they exclaimed. They suddenly charged for the door, but Tomoyo blocked their way.

"Are you going to change another Card?" the girl asked.

"I can sense Clow, so it looks like it," said Sakura.

"Well then," murmured Tomoyo. She then grabbed her backpack, reached in, and procured her special drone. It floated off her hand and fixated upon Sakura. "I upgraded it, so it has double its top speed and quadruple the range," she exclaimed. Reaching back into the bag, she added, "And that isn't all."

Out came a clothing bag, and Sakura's heart sank in her

chest.

* * *

Had Xiaolang's senses been less attuned, he'd have received Sakura's phone call with mirth. He'd spent most of the day smiling at the memory of his dance with her. He hadn't been able to recall a time when he'd been in a better mood.

Then he sensed the presence of Clow. He was already out the door with a pocket full of paper charms by the time he got Sakura's call.

"I sense it!" he yelled. He raced up to the top of his building, and extended his senses outward over the city. He threaded his tendrils of awareness across every building and structure within his reach. He zoned in on the stench of his ancestor, the source of his Number One's pain. Then he caught it, within the aetheric flow. His attention went southward.

"Outa City, Haneda, I think," he said into his phone.

"I think so too," said Sakura, who seemed to be struggling with something on the other end.

"Are you alright?" asked Xiaolang.

"I'm fine, I'll meet you there," the girl blurted. The call ended.

Xiaolang whipped into action. He leapt off the roof and ascended a drainpipe into the alleyway. Then he raced across the street, leapt clean across the train-tracks near Yoyogi-Hachiman station. With his magic, he increased his speed such that no one would recognise him as he dashed past. He cleared Yoyogi Park in ten seconds flat, and vaulted onto the roof of a train heading southward from Shibuya. He train hopped the whole way down south into Outa City, until he reached Otorii Station.

Xiaolang raced out of the station, and looked around. Anyone who noticed him saw an out-of-breath Chinese guy glancing around manically in the middle of the road. He couldn't localise the source of Clow's signature, but knew it was close.

"Xiaolang!" came a heavenly voice from above. Xiaolang turned to see Kero's winged-lion form swoop in from the west, Tomoyo and Sakura riding on his back. His eyes bugged out in horror. He glanced around, seeing that everyone was going about their business despite the magical creature in their midst.

As Kero came into land, Sakura extended her wand and commanded, "Include him amid our subterfuge, Maya!" The Maya Card (which used to be Illusion) enveloped him. Nearby, he heard some people mutter, "Where did that weirdo go?"

"You've gotten stronger," he said, his voice full of pride. He finally looked at the girl, and almost fainted. The costume looked a little like the one she wore for the Final Judgement, but it was different. The pink shorts were slightly darker, and reached just below sthe knees. The overcoat seemed melded into them, and appeared to be composed of tough-yet-comfortable fabric. The most obvious feature was the bright yellow star emblazoned on her chest.

"It's my best one yet!" exclaimed Tomoyo. She piloted her drone around them and snapped dozens of pictures.

"Well, let's make it count," said Kero.

"Kerberus, what about Yue?" asked Xiaolang.

"Dumbass is on his way," said Kero.

"We can't wait," yelled Xiaolang. He glanced at Sakura. "Let's find whoever this Clow impostor is."

"Definitely," returned Sakura.

They glanced about, extending their senses to localise the source of Clow's signature.

"I can't localise where he is," said Xiaolang. "But he's nearby."

"It's like he's everywhere," said Sakura.

Xiaolang's gaze went to the tall yellow building beside the road.

"Higher ground," he said.

Sakura caught his meaning instantly, and followed him. She drew a Card and said, "Put a spring in my feet, Launch!" Wings appeared on her ankles, and she rocketed into the air. Xiaolang rode on a gust of wind from a paper charm, while Tomoyo mounted Kero and flew to the top of the building. From there, they glanced across the Tokyo skyline, and extended their senses as far as they could. Yet, it still felt as if Clow was everywhere.

Wind blew in from the northwest, and Sakura glanced in that direction to see Yue, holding Touya in his arms. Her heart skipped a beat.

"Yue! Why did you bring him?" she asked, her wand held behind her back reflexively.

"I wanna see this myself," said Touya. He glanced at the group. He looked at Kero and didn't even bat an eye. "Just once, I wanna see!"

Sakura looked at him nervously, and recalled his sacrifice for her.

I might as well, she concluded.

"Don't get in the way," said Xiaolang.

"Yue, we can't lock on the signature," said Kero.

Yue closed his eyes, and brought his full power into focus. He extended his senses outward, feeling through the aether for where the sensation was strongest. Yet he felt the same intensity everywhere.

Xiaolang saw the mounting worry in Sakura's face at repeated failure. He stepped forward and took her hand.

"We can resonate," he said. "Just like you do with the Cards. If we do that, we can make our senses even stronger. We might be able to sense him then."

Kero's eyes lit up. "Brat's on to somethin' there!" He moved to Sakura's side, and she placed a hand on his back. Yue placed a hand on Sakura's shoulder, and they all exchanged glances.

Meanwhile, Tomoyo panned the drone around them, and giggled to Touya, "It's like they're superheroes, isn't it?"

The quartet of magical beings closed their eyes, slowed their breathing, and reached out to each other through the aether. Their bodies started to shimmer with blue light. Their minds echoed with a resounding chorus: "Soul Resonance."

In that instant, the entire city shrunk within reach of their senses. They could sense the shape and movement of every object within the city, the flow of air in every breath, the energy in every particle. Their combined magical radar burst outward in a sweeping beam through the aether, scanning for the slightest betrayal of their quarry.

There, to the southeast, they sensed it.

"Uh, Sakura," said Touya nervously as they broke their resonance. He pointed to the southeast, from where they sensed the strongest presence of Clow. "There wasn't a storm forecast today," he intoned.

Sakura's eyes widened as a massive storm front materialised. It cast shadows across the entire Chiba region, rays of light feebly seeping through the blanket and scintillating through heavy rain. Flashes of light heralded the sounds of thunder, rumbling across the city like the roar of an unstoppable beast.

"That's not an ordinary storm! That's Clow's magic," she exclaimed.

The people of Tokyo gazed upward with fear and alarm, which clouded Sakura's senses like tear gas. She felt Xiaolang's hand grip hers, bringing her focus to the task at hand.

"Sakura, look!" yelled Kero. Yue pointed toward a dot within the cloud.

A flash of lightning revealed it to be a landing aircraft, caught in the storm. Sakura was utterly petrified with fear as she gripped the Star Wand. She glanced around in a panic, and saw Kero, Yue, and Xiaolang. She turned around and saw Tomoyo and Touya, bewildered expressions greeting her own gaze.

They're one's I have to protect, she decided. *I won't fail!*

"Kero! Yue! You're with me!" she bellowed. "Xiaolang, look after Tomoyo and Touya."

"Got it," replied Xiaolang.

Sakura procured an inert Clow Card and held it high. She uttered her incantation, and the Fly Card transformed in a mesmerising flash. She touched her wand to it and proclaimed, "Grant me the fastest wings, Flight!"

The Card dematerialised into four ribbons of energy that encircled her. They materialised into a pair of primary wings on her shoulders with a set of secondary wings on her lower back. She spread them outwards with a deep breath to steel her nerves and recover her strength. She turned around to see looks of amazement and pride on her friends' faces.

"I'll be back," she said.

The three angelic beings took flight, and darted through the air toward the cloud. As they drew near, they started to feel the torrents on the outskirts of the storm. Sakura pushed all her effort into the resonance link with the Flight Card. Somehow, she remained stable in the face of the mounting turbulence. She focused on the plane, which pitched violently in the storm. A red flash burst from the starboard engine.

"They're in trouble," exclaimed Kero, barely audible over the storm.

Sakura drew another Card and yelled, "Show me the meaning of haste! Gale!" The Card shimmered, and a great gust of wind locked under their wings. The plane came in much faster, and they landed on its fuselage. Sakura cast out the Aqua Card in an effort to snuff the engine fire, but it only made more smoke.

The hairs on her body stood on end. She could sense the incoming lightning strike. Without a thought, she cast out a Card and yelled, "Make this plane a lightning rod, Spark!" She felt an electric shock sear through her legs as the fuselage became electrified, and the lightning skirted around it. The force from the discharge blew Sakura off her feet, and the aircraft pitched again, throwing her off the edge.

She fell into Yue's waiting grip. She looked into his face and saw Yukito's smile.

"I made a promise," said Yue. He then sped back to the plane, where Kero unleashed fireballs to disperse any electrical discharge.

Sakura gripped the plane's tailfin to steady herself, and looked at the burning engine. Rain continued to hound her.

There's water everywhere, but the fire won't go out, she pondered amid the tumult. Then she had an epiphany.

She cast out a Card, "Still these fires, Flare!" The Card morphed into a fiery serpent, which cast out a flood of steam against the rain. It slithered into the engine, and the fires died down. The engine continued to whine and growl through the storm, until it finally gave out.

"Watch out!" screamed Kero, his wings ruffling.

The plane suddenly tipped downward, a mighty whorl from within the storm blasting its tail upward. Sakura tumbled through the air and landed on Kero's back. She glanced over in horror to see the plane plummeting.

"No!" she screamed. Her wings sprouted from her back and she went into a nosedive. She straightened out to streamline herself, and summoned every ounce of her energy into her speed. Smoke from the engine clouded her eyes, and she squeezed them shut. She reached out with her magical senses to guide her to the plane.

Then she procured a Card.

Please work!

"Right this skewed ship, Gale!" she yelled.

The Card generated a forceful draft, which locked onto the plane's guide-flaps and jerked them in just the right way. Then with an otherworldly shriek, Gale thrust its form into the underside of the fuselage. The aircraft pulled out of its nosedive to Sakura's delight. She held her wand tightly, ignoring her fatigue, and controlled Gale's motions.

She guided the wind under the aircraft's wings to keep it aloft.

Sakura glanced around for a safe landing spot, and saw the main runway of Tokyo Haneda to the north. Keeping her mind focused on Gale's movements, she advanced toward the front of the plane. She knocked on the windshield, frightening the already befuddled pilots.

"Go north!" she yelled. They couldn't hear her.

"Allow me, Master," said Spark in her mind. The Card activated, and a yellow glowing mouthpiece materialised before her. She repeated her demand, which came through the cockpit radio. The pilots nervously capitulated, and veered north toward the runway.

Sakura slowly guided them downward. They drew closer to the ground, until one of the pilots exclaimed, "The brake flaps aren't working. We're coming in too fast!"

Sakura had one last trick up her sleeve. She drew a Card. "Soften the earth before me, Gaia!"

The tarmac runway crumbled into dust and loam, which the plane struck with a dull slurp. It bounced, throwing Sakura into the air only to be caught, once again, by Yue. She continued to administer Gale, which guided more wind into the path of the crashing airliner, until it finally came to rest.

Sakura, Yue, and Kero set down on the ground nearby. She raced forward, eager to see if the passengers were safe. She tapped on the windshield, now opaque with dirt and grime, but received no response.

Kero drew near and said, "I can't sense any movement inside." As Yue created a blade out of energy to cut through the cabin doors, Kero noticed the absence of any rescue crews. He listened for ambulances, or even the movement of the air traffic controllers in the towers nearby.

"I ain't sensin' movement anywhere," he intoned.

Yue finished hacking a hole in the cabin, and Sakura

climbed inside. Everyone in the cabin was unconscious, and would not respond even when she screamed.

"Sakura, we got a problem," said Kero.

She emerged to find them staring up at the sky.

"What's the matter?" she asked. She glanced up and saw a dark sky. "So what? It was a storm, right?"

"No," said Yue. "The rain stopped. There's no thunder."

"No stars," mumbled Kero.

Sakura looked harder, and realised the same thing. The sky had disappeared.

Her neck hairs prickled with the sound of crackling embers. She glanced over and saw that damaged engine. Time seemed to slow to a crawl. In that instant, she saw a line of fire scamper its way across the ground toward a puddle of foul-smelling liquid.

Fuel ...

That ember hit the puddle. There was a sudden and violent flash. A torrent of panic and desperation flooded Sakura's mind, such that all she could think of was life. Her every experience flashed before her very eyes.

Her mother's face appeared before her, and she whispered, "Not yet."

Sakura's eyes flew open, and she saw the topaz star within her wand spinning madly. Before her was a sphere of fiery energy, held in place by a force field. A Card hung in the air before her, glimmering with the signs of activation. Emblazoned upon it was the word 'Guard.'

"Without an incantation!" exclaimed Yue.

"Sakura! Hold your focus!" yelled Kero.

Sakura pushed aside her surprise and directed her mind to containing the blast within the force field. Then, she started to twirl her wand in the air. The sphere of fire twirled with her. With a flick of her wrist, the sphere flew into the air, far above the wrecked plane, and exploded.

Exhausted and overwhelmed with adrenaline, Sakura fell to her knees. Yue and Kero raced to her side, and shouldered their tired Master. But they knew it wasn't over yet. A completely black sky loomed overhead.

A one-man round of applause pierced the silence.

The trio glanced toward the terminal building, and saw a single man walking toward them. He clapped with increasing excitement and jubilation. The pride was evident on his face as he stepped into the light of the runway.

"I ain't seen a show like that in a long while, quine," exclaimed the man with a thick Scottish accent.

Sakura froze, as did Yue and Kero. The sensation of Clow's presence no longer surrounded them, but was centred entirely on the man in front of them. He gave that wide smile Sakura had expected to see every day in English class.

"Eriol?" she whispered.

"Aye," said Eriol, grinning like the prime suspect in a murder case.

"But this presence," mumbled Kero.

The man glanced at the winged lion, unfazed by his appearance. In fact, he seemed like he was greeting an old friend. He said, "Kerberus, it's been so long." He glanced at Yue, and his expression softened. "Me little Moon, Yue."

"What is this?" asked Sakura breathlessly. "How do you know Kero and Yue?"

"Ya see, quine," said Eriol. "In this life, I'm Eriol Lamperouge, a minted-as-feck Scotsman from Aberdeen." He reached down his shirt and procured a key, its handle in the shape of the sun. Yue and Kero gasped in befuddled amazement.

"A Shadow Key," they muttered.

Eriol went on, in fluent Japanese, "But in my past life, I was known as Clow Reed."

16 | Shadow Spell

The streets of Outa City were alight with gasps and concerned faces. Every eye was fixated on the plane, trapped in the storm. Few were close enough to notice the three winged creatures flitting about it, and their effort to keep it from crashing.

Xiaolang, Touya, and Tomoyo sprinted down the street toward Tokyo Haneda Airport. From a distance, they could see the aircraft pitch and trace a long arc from the south toward the airport. A long trail of fire and soot flew from its wing, only to be ripped apart in the fierce winds of the storm.

The storm started to subside as the plane descended. It disappeared behind the skyline, and a dull thud rippled through the ground. People shrieked as a plume of dirt flew above the rooftops where the aircraft struck the tarmac, and all feared the worst.

"Is she?" asked Touya in a panic. Tomoyo gasped.

Xiaolang reached out through the aether, and sensed Sakura's soul. It was still very much alive and kicking, though absolutely soaked in fear and fatigue.

"She's fine," he said. "We need to get to the tarmac as soon as possible."

Tomoyo started to falter. She clutched her chest and wheezed.

"We can't stop, Daidouji," said Xiaolang.

Touya stepped in front of her and yelled, "Hop on!"

Tomoyo moved to mount Touya's shoulders, before suddenly collapsing against his back. Touya cradled her to the ground, and growled with vexations. Xiaolang held his hand over her forehead, but could not sense any injury.

"She's asleep," he said, equally befuddled.

"What the Hell?" exclaimed Touya. He then clutched his own chest, as did several people nearby. Few managed to pant expressions of bewilderment before their legs gave out.

Xiaolang glanced around as everyone on the bustling street collapsed like dominoes. He felt a twinge of fatigue overtake him as well, and he fell to his knees. He grit his teeth and clenched his fist as he wondered what was going on. He glanced up, and saw the sun disappear.

An eclipse?

He squinted a little, and saw the tendrils of darkness bleed across the sky.

"That's no eclipse," he growled. He pushed through the fatigue demanding that he sleep, and extended his senses. "This is Clow's magic!"

Visions of Sakura in peril overcame him, and he drew strength from them. He focused his mind, summoned every ounce of his magical power, and forced himself to stand. He gazed down at Tomoyo and Touya, and said, "I'll look after her."

Then he turned and raced toward the airport, where the signature of Clow Reed had become the strongest.

* * *

Eriol's grin widened menacingly as his Shadow Key floated before him. It glistened in the darkness as he uttered an incantation that made Sakura's hair stand on end:

> *Key who conceals the Magic of Shadow,*
> *Ye who is more than ye seems:*
> *I command thee to bestow*

The power ye deems.
Let us fulfil our vow
In time's great streams ... Release!

The key dematerialised with an otherworldly screech. It then grew to the length of Eriol's arm reach, and became a majestic golden staff. The symbol of the Sun adorned one end, the Moon the other.

"Not bad, innit?" he chirped.

"What do you mean, you're Clow Reed?" exclaimed Sakura. "I saw Clow! He was an old Chinese man."

Eriol cackled, "Past life, quine! Clow had himself reborn as li'l ol' me. Bit of a tosser, if ya ask me. But a life's a life, eh?"

"Must've been you who made that storm what almost drown'd us," said Kero. "Ya almost killed Sakura. Why?"

"Forget that!" screamed Yue as he advanced upon the Scotsman. "Why did you reincarnate, Clow? Why tell us you were going to die and leave us?" Tears escaped the silver angel's eyes as he bellowed, "Why did you make me choose a new Master?!"

"Hoora good questions!" chuckled Eriol as he twirled his wand. "But I'll only answer if you can defeat me."

"So be it," growled Yue.

"You always were a butthole, Clow," barked Kero.

With a flourish, Yue materialised a sword of light, while Kero bared his claws. They raced forward, ignoring the pleas of their Master, and engaged Eriol. With a face as casual as if he were pouring some tea, Eriol twirled his staff and diverted Yue's sword. He then swatted away Kero's paw swipes and nimbly dodged the lion's lunge. He held his staff behind his back to block Yue's blow, and kicked at Yue's knees with expert precision.

"Oooh, Yue, surely you can do better," he taunted.

Yue fumed and pressed his attack. His speed increased, but Eriol was faster. The wizard's staff appeared in the path of Yue's every blow, and there wasn't even a blur of motion to precede it. Eriol swivelled and swatted Yue's temple with his staff. He then released the staff and delivered a volley of punches up and down Yue's torso, before kicking his staff with his heel, catching it behind his back, and bringing the full force of his weapon against Yue's side.

Yue toppled to the ground, gripping his stomach.

"Clow!" roared Kero. The lion crouched low, and his eyes glow a deep red. From his throat burst a barrage of fire, aimed directly at Eriol's head. The Scotsman nonchalantly held out his staff, and the Sun emblem shimmered. The fire blast met a force field that glimmered and thrummed in the air about him. Kero quickly ran out of breath and he panted with frustration. Eriol's staff glowed a bright red, and with a loud ping unleashed a bolt of energy that floored the winged lion.

"Kero!" screeched Sakura. She raced toward her unconscious friend and tried in vain to rouse him. She glared at Eriol, tears of betrayal welling up. Eriol returned little more than his usual polite smile.

Meanwhile, Yue pulled himself to his feet. Scuffmarks marred his changsham robe and normally pristine face. His silver reptilian eyes glistened with rage as he summoned a bow and arrow into his hand. He loosed the arrow, only for Eriol to flick it back at him, without even diverting his gaze from Sakura. The arrow skewered Yue's shoulder, and he hit the ground with an agonised shriek.

"Stop it!" screamed Sakura. "Why are you doing this, Eriol? Aren't we friends?"

Eriol just chuckled and shrugged. "Same reason I started that storm, made ya fimo shisa big and alive, turned ya boyfriend into a puppet and made him fight ya, set up ya bro in that movie, and knocked a'body out here."

"That was all you?" Sakura whispered. "You came to Japan just to torture me?" Eriol nodded excitedly, as if it were something to be wonderfully proud of. "Why?" cried Sakura.

"Defeat me, and find out," said Eriol.

Suddenly, the Scotsman flew through the air and landed headfirst in the nearby plane wreck. Sakura only had a split second to notice, but was sure she'd seen a nice imprint of a foot in Eriol's back. Befuddled, she glanced back to where he'd stood, and saw Xiaolang. Waves of magical energy permeated his body, fuelled by what had to be pure rage.

"There! Consider yourself defeated!" barked the boy.

"Xiaolang! Where are Tomoyo and Big Brother?" asked Sakura.

"Passed out back in the city," said Xiaolang. "The sky started to go dark and they collapsed. I'm betting it's because of him. It almost got me too, but I managed to stay awake with my magic."

Sakura's heart ached as she thought of Touya lying unconscious in a dead city.

All because he gave Yue his power, she thought.

Eriol clumsily rolled off the wreck and looked around. He didn't have a scratch on his body. That only made Xiaolang madder.

"Jings!" exclaimed Eriol as he summoned his staff into his hand. "I have never been hit so hard in my life … *lives!* You've gotten stronger, Coyote!"

"So you know my codename," retorted Xiaolang. "Mother anticipated Clow'd reincarnate, but she expected it to be a Chinese man."

"That's racist, don't ya think?" chirped the Scotsman.

"Who cares!" barked Xiaolang. "I defeated you. So why is it still dark?"

"Oh! Pfft!" exclaimed Eriol, swatting his own head. "I should have said, 'Defeat me *spell.*'" He glanced at Sakura with a genuine apology. "Sorry, quine, that's my mistake."

Sakura trembled as she gripped the Star Wand. She glanced at the sky around her. The pitch-blackness made her sick to her stomach, and her legs almost gave out. She glanced between Eriol and Xiaolang.

"How do I do it?" she asked.

Xiaolang looked up, but couldn't think of a way.

"I don't even know what spell this is," he replied.

"Ya know, you two're great students," said Eriol. "But you're bloody stupid." He fixed his gaze on Xiaolang. "I'll leave Sakura to figure it out."

In the blink of an eye, Eriol crossed the distance between him and Xiaolang, and launched the boy clear across the tarmac. Xiaolang managed to slow his flight just enough to survive the impact, and pulled himself up. Blood trickled from his mouth and forehead, and scrapes ran down his hands and wrists. He pushed himself off the ground, motivated by frustration and months of pent up irritation. He sensed Eriol advancing upon him from behind.

I don't need to hold back now, he thought gleefully.

With a deep breath, he gathered all his power into his hands. He spread his arms wide, and then slammed his palms together. Light flashed from within his hands as if a star were forming between them. Then he prised them apart, and the energy between them formed a long, elegant Chinese jian. He gripped the sword by the handle just as Eriol came within reach.

Xiaolang swivelled and slashed at his attacker with a deafening, unbelievably satisfying roar. The blade struck Eriol's staff with a deafening clang that shocked the Scotsman. He fell backward onto the tarmac and rolled to a stop. He came to his feet, his staff still ringing from the blow, and smiled with utter admiration. Xiaolang marched toward him, the magical energy about his body howling like a wolf.

"Spank me!" exclaimed Eriol. "You're truly a testament to your namesake, Coyote!"

"Let's go, limey!" barked Xiaolang.

He advanced, his blade glowing with the full force of his magic. Eriol twirled his staff, deflecting and swatting away every single blow. But with each strike, the Scotsman faltered. The staff vibrated louder and louder, until the entire airport echoed with the ring. It's thrumming pulsated up Eriol's arm and weakened his grip. He backed away from Xiaolang, twirled the staff clumsily and thrust it into the ground, which lit up with a crash. A shockwave burst from it, and threw Xiaolang back.

Xiaolang back flipped and drew a paper charm. He pressed it to his blade and proclaimed, *"Huǒ shén zhāolái!"* The sword ignited with a searing fire. Then, he bounded forward.

Eriol launched himself from the ground to meet the boy. Their weapons locked, and the air around them exploded like a solar flare. The Scotsman raised his staff, and summoned a volley of energetic shards. Xiaolang raced headfirst into the barrage, swatting and deflecting each one that came his way, until he came within reach of his grinning foe.

Their weapons locked once more, and Xiaolang pressed against Eriol. He channelled all his fury into his attack, and it fuelled his magical power. That power burst from his sword in vibrant flames that licked menacingly at Eriol's defences.

Xiaolang locked eyes with Eriol. The Scotsman looked like he was having a hard time maintaining his defence. He started to buckle under the assault.

"So much for the reincarnation of Clow Reed," barked Xiaolang with a sneer.

Eriol stopped shaking, and his grin returned with a vengeance. His staff started to glimmer at the intersection with Xiaolang's jian.

"You're strong, Coyote," he said. "But you've got a ways to go yet."

Xiaolang felt his energy drain. The fire of his blade diminished into subtle embers, only to be swallowed by Eriol's staff. All that remained between them was that small ball of light where their weapons touched.

With a raucous clang, that light burst and sent Xiaolang

flying through the air, knocked unconscious by the sorcerer's counter. A pillow of wind broke his fall, cast out by a desperate, bewildered Sakura.

Tears had carved a path down her dirty face. She wiped them away, only to leave muddy smears that dried on her hot flushed cheeks. Eriol returned little more than his usual smile. He looked as if he were watching an amazing action movie, just itching for the climax.

I have to defeat his spell, thought Sakura. *But I don't want to hurt him.*

She cast out the Gaia Card, which caused a fissure to erupt beneath Eriol. He simply darted out of the way. She then sent out Bloom and Forest, which looped around his ankles to hold him in place. Eriol just touched his staff to the ground, and the roots disintegrated. He looked annoyed. Sakura summoned a lightning bolt, which he shrugged off. Then she sent a barrage of shadowy spines that dinged harmlessly off his defences.

"C'mon, Sakura," he moaned.

Sakura cast out Gale and Aqua, and threw all her strength into the resonance link. Tendrils of wind and water spiralled about her foe. Eriol just rolled his eyes.

"Haud it now, aye?" he mumbled. The tendrils tore at him more and more desperately. He snatched his arm out of the tumult and swiped with his staff. The Cards retreated from his yawp and withdrew to their exhausted Master. Eriol threw his hands up in dismay. "What is wrong with you?" he exclaimed. "Defeat me spell!"

"I don't know how!" cried Sakura.

"Well, you'd better figure it out, quine," replied Eriol. "It's getting close to night. You don't beat the spell by then, you'll really be pooched."

"What?" asked Sakura.

"Them people in the city won't wake up," said Eriol with an exasperated expression. He looked like her father whenever he chided her for not finishing her homework. "You need to break the spell, or they'll sleep forever."

"No!" cried Sakura. She fell to her knees helplessly. "Why are you doing this, Eriol? What did I do to you?"

"Break the spell, and I'll tell you," said Eriol firmly. His fingers tapped his staff impatiently.

Sakura buried her face in her hands.

I don't know what to do. I've used all the Cards I can think of, but nothing can beat him. Not even Yue or Xiaolang could beat him. Even when I put all my power into the Cards, nothing works.

She felt a paw on her shoulder. Kero pushed himself to his feet beside her and looked into her eyes.

"Sakura, there's still two more Cards," he stammered.

Yue appeared next to them and said, "One of those Cards can banish this darkness, right?"

Sakura looked at them dumbfounded. A moment of lucidity brought her the answer, and she was stunned that it hadn't occurred to her sooner. She procured the Light Card. The woman in white with black outline looked dull, as if in a sleep as deep as death. She uttered the incantation to transform it, but nothing happened.

"Ooh-eeh, you're dense, quine," droned Eriol as he twirled his staff.

"Shut up, Clow!" roared Kero. He and Yue focused on Sakura. "Think, Sakura, what did Light ask you when you first met?"

"It was a riddle to catching it," said Yue.

Sakura thought back to that moment, standing on a hill just south of Mount Kumoso. Enveloped in darkness, she recalled the words uttered to her by the Light.

The Light, and what, are two sides of the same coin?

"I need to change Light and Dark at the same time!" she exclaimed. Excitedly, she withdrew the Dark Card and prepared to recite the incantation a second time. Yue put his hand on her wand and drew her gaze.

"You alone won't be enough," he said. "The creation of those Cards almost killed Clow, for they are the Master Cards of the deck."

"Ya need more power," said Kero. Before panic and

dismay could set in, the winged lion added, "Use us."

"What do you mean?" asked Sakura.

Her guardians stepped back and faced her.

"Kerberus and I will merge with the Star Wand," Yue explained. "That will augment your powers enough to transform the Cards."

"You better watch it, me cannie Yue," said Eriol. "If Sakura can't change the Cards …" He gestured for them to tell her.

Kero huffed, "He's *worse* than Clow." He looked to Sakura with a pained expression. "If ya can't change 'em, then we won't come outta the wand."

"We shall remain dormant within the staff, forever," said Yue.

"No!" screamed Sakura. She threw her arms around Kero and cried, "I can't let that happen! There has to be another way!"

She felt Kero's paw encircle her, and Yue's hand caress her hair. She looked at both of them.

"See? Didn't I pick a good Master?" said Kero to Yue.

Yue harrumphed. "She's certainly less of a headache than Clow."

"I don't want you to disappear," Sakura sobbed.

"We won't," said Kero resolutely. "Ya'll change 'em Cards in no time, eh?"

Yue cut off Sakura's pessimistic retort and said, "Don't forget your invincible spell."

The voice of Sakura's mother echoed in her mind and she recited, "I'll definitely be alright."

She forced herself to remember those words. They gave her the strength to make her legs stop shaking. She made them echo in her mind as she proclaimed, "Sun and Moon, transfer thy essence to the wand and grant me strength."

She felt their souls resonating, thrumming a transcendent tone through their link. Before her, their forms disintegrated into swirling wisps of gold and silver light. They encircled the wand and spiralled inward toward its hull. The wand grew to double its length. The star upon its tip grew in size and vibrancy, until it was encircled by resplendent wings and guarded by the Sun and Msoon.

The Light and Dark Cards floated above her. She directed her staff at them, and drew a deep breath.

I'll definitely be alright.

She threw all her mental energy into transforming the Cards. The edges of the Cards started to glisten, and that light grew inwards slowly.

I can do it!

Sakura pushed more energy through the resonance link. A maelstrom of noise grew around her, and bright mist girdled her. She felt the Cards push back, as if they wished to remain comatose. The darkness of the sky fell upon her until she could see nothing more than the Cards themselves. Their light started to fade.

Panic flooded her consciousness. She began to falter in the wake of mounting fatigue. Images of Tomoyo, Touya, Franklin, and all her friends, asleep forever, ruptured her focus and she fell to her knees.

No! I can't fail! I can't fail them again! My friends and my family! They'll be gone forever!

A pair of hands gripped hers and hoisted her to her feet. She opened her eyes and saw a pair of amber orbs.

"Xiaolang!" she cried.

"We're not done yet," he yelled over the din. He looked almost ready to keel over. But he stood strong. "I've still got some magic left. We can do this together."

Sakura gave it no second thought, and reached out to him through the resonance link. She felt his power surge through her.

"This is it," she exclaimed, almost cockily.

"It's show time, Cardcaptor!" bellowed Xiaolang.

Together, they gazed up at the Cards, still shimmering on the verge of reincarnation. As one voice, they roared the incantation:

Cards of Clow, thy magic innate,
Discard thy forms and reincarnate.
Ye serve, hence, under a new Master:
Sakura of the Shining Star!

In an instant, the Cards morphed into their new forms. Light became Lucis and Dark became Noctis. They issued forth a spiralling column of light and dark, which shot into the sky with all the force of an incoming meteorite. They ripped apart the mass of shadowy matter that was Eriol's spell, and filled the sky with mesmerising twilight. Black and white balls of energy trickled downwards like a gentle snowfall.

All that remained was the fading afternoon light.

Sakura let out a shriek of relief, and threw her arms around Xiaolang. Between them, the staff shrunk to its regular size. Kero and Yue rematerialized from their pure energetic forms. But they were different.

Yue's changsham had become brighter, with a greater array of blue and white shades. There was certainly more majesty to the patterns woven into his robes.

Kero's build looked more muscular. His armour plates shone with greater vibrancy, and his fur glimmered as if the sun itself shone through his flesh.

"You look amazing!" exclaimed Sakura.

"Well, now that all the Cards have changed, so too have we," said Yue.

"Now, you well and truly are our Master," said Kero.

Sakura glanced at Xiaolang, who returned only an expression of pride.

The group heard the sound of a crumpling body. They looked over and saw Eriol on his knees. His staff was gone, and his expression was utterly perplexing. He was smiling, most ecstatically.

"Yes!" he screamed joyously. He scrambled to his feet, pushed past the bewildered guardians and Xiaolang, and threw his arms around Sakura. He lifted her into the air and squeezed her. "You did it, quine! You really did it!" He dropped her to the ground and thrust his fingers to the sky. "In your face, Clow, you ruddy bastard! In your face!"

"The heck's goin' on?" exclaimed Kero.

Yue stepped forward, and readied himself for another fight. Eriol waved him off.

"Never mind, Yue," he panted. "I'm done with all that."

"You said you'd answer our questions if we defeated your spell," said Yue, rage overshadowing his confusion. "Explain yourself, Clow."

Eriol wiped away a few tears and said, "That I did, m'boy. That I did." He looked around in a fit of concern and added, "But prob'ly not here. People're wakin' up soon. We'd better skedaddle."

"Where to?" asked Xiaolang, reflexively holding Sakura close.

Eriol clapped his hands, and the world around them vanished.

17 | Celebration

The house before them looked familiar. In the fading afternoon light, it was difficult to make out the colours of the roof and outer walls. It was only when Sakura squinted that she realised she was standing in front of Eriol's mansion.

The Scotsman sighed, "Well then, anyone up for some snashters?" He pointed to Sakura's left and chortled, "Kerberus, I know you'll like some, eh?"

Sakura looked to her left and saw Kero's teddy bear form. He looked just as surprised as she. To her right stood Yukito, absolutely mystified. Xiaolang, Tomoyo, and Touya stood equally perplexed nearby.

"Tomoyo, Big Brother, are you alright?" she asked, rushing to them. She checked them over.

"We're fine," said Tomoyo.

"But how did we get here?" asked Touya. "Last I remember, I was runnin' with the creep to the airport."

"Yeah, that was my bad," said Eriol, his Japanese far more fluent than Sakura remembered. He beckoned them into the house, but they all remained immobile. "C'mon, let's have some tea," he exclaimed. Every face but Tomoyo and Touya regarded him with apprehension. Understandable, since he'd tortured all of them and was now being all smiley. He sighed, "It's done now. No more magic from me, I promise. I've healed all your wounds, which I'm sorry about. And I said I'd explain everything. So, come in."

Sakura moved to follow Yukito, Kero, and Xiaolang. Tomoyo grabbed her hand and asked, "Wait, Mister Lamperouge has magic? Since when?"

Sakura swallowed and said, "I'll explain on the way."

She detailed the whole battle between her and Eriol, including the transformation of the final Cards. Tomoyo gasped when Sakura explained who Eriol claimed to be. Touya, on the other hand, just remained stoic.

Eriol led the group through the familiar house. He had a definite spring in his step as he opened the door to the dining room, and ushered them in. Jaws dropped at the sight of the feast resting on the table. Not only had tea been laid out, but also a fine assortment of finger-food, including Sakura's favourite takoyaki. Kero was practically hypnotised by the Modern-Yaki served at a seat labelled just for him.

"Please, have a seat," said their host, his smile warm and genuine.

Kero was already won over, and practically dove into his meal. Everyone else took seats where they had been labelled. Eriol took a seat at the head of the table next to Sakura and motioned for them to serve themselves.

Sakura took a placid sip of tea and asked, "So, what was the whole thing about?"

"Yeah!" barked Kero, spewing pastry and noodle crumbs everywhere. "Start talkin', Scottie!"

Eriol chortled as he poured some milk into his tea and drank a bit. "Aye, where to begin, eh?" He looked like he was recovering from an arduous hike up Mount Everest. "Long ago, Clow Reed created the Cards."

"Heard this story!" barked Kero.

"Not everyone, Kerberus," said Eriol.

Sakura chided Kero for interrupting and motioned for Eriol to continue.

"Clow Reed'd lived for yonks, and watched the world

go through a lot of strife. There were those in Asia who believed havin' the biggest stick was the best way to peace. But that just created more pain. Then there were those in Europe who thought bein' indestructible would bring peace. But that just made monsters of 'em all. There were those from the ancient world, still bidin' now, who figured they had to kill off the bad eggs. But that just rotted more eggs.

"Clow thought of something different. He thought, maybe, that the way to peace wasn't to cull the course or the tadgers, or bein' unkillable or unbeatable. He figured that, if there was somethin' to encourage people to be good, while managin' the bad in a sensible manner, maybe that'd do the trick. So he made the Clow Cards. Whoever wielded them had the power to make the world a better place. Too bad, though. He died before the Cards could reach their full power."

Yukito harrumphed as he hoed into a hefty serving of Eriol's offerings.

"Yue wasn't too pleased about that," he said.

"Of course not," said Tomoyo. "I'd be devastated if it was Mom."

"Worse if she announced it on the day," said Eriol. "That's what Clow did to our two little friends here."

Kero licked his plate clean, and plonked down like a little ball. "I thought he was jokin' back when."

"So that's why he made the book, then?" asked Sakura.

"He left it to me to pick a candidate for a new Master," said Kero. "Yue had to decide."

"Come now, Kerberus," said Yukito through a mouthful of sushi. "Even I know Clow planned for everything." He eyed Eriol. "Right?"

Sakura glanced at Eriol, befuddled at their meaning.

"On the day of his death, Clow looked into the future," said Eriol. "He saw you, Sakura. He decided that you should be the one to carry on his legacy and fulfil his dream. He manufactured every single coincidence so that the Cards would fall into your care. He then sent me, imbued with his memories and all his magical power, to guide you on this final step."

"To change the Cards into her own," interjected Touya. "It's also why I gave up my power, right? All part of this Clow Reed's game?"

Eriol shrugged in bewilderment. "There are a lot of things Clow couldn't have predicted." His gaze darted between Yukito and Touya. Then he looked at Tomoyo, before eying Xiaolang. He finally looked at Sakura, clearly having trouble processing everything.

"Why didn't you just tell me when we first met?" asked Sakura. "It could have been so much easier."

"My dear Sakura, triumph is never achieved easily," said Eriol. "Think of how much stronger you are, and what a better position you're in, thanks to my meddlin'."

Sakura looked around the table. She glanced at Tomoyo, and recalled her best friend's revelation out the front of the same mansion in which she stood. She glanced at Yukito, and, although the feeling was bittersweet, she felt truly happy that Touya had a Number One of his own.

Then she looked at Xiaolang.

The first man I danced with.

The thought made her cheeks burn.

"I do feel I should apologise for a few things though," said Eriol, shame evident in his gaze. "I had orchestrated the movie shoot to create another opportunity to change a Card. I suspected it would lead to Mister Kinomoto giving up his powers to Yue. But I never thought it would lead you down a path where you almost died trying to change all the Cards. I was created specifically for that purpose." He looked straight into Sakura's eyes. "I am truly sorry, Sakura."

Sakura's expression softened. Having considered every experience she'd had over the last few months, she could not be mad at the boy. She reached out and grabbed his hand.

"Thanks for pushing me in just the right way," she said.

Kero floated into the air and bellowed, "Well then, now that all that crap is out of the way, we're havin' a party to celebrate changin' all the Cards!"

Everyone backed away from the table as Kero tackled at a sstack of marshmallow and caramel puffs. The teddy bear's mouth unhinged like a snake and devoured the entire serving, before spitting out the glass cups in which they'd been served. He looked to his left and saw Touya shooting a disgusted expression his way.

"The heck're you lookin' at!" snapped the Beast of the Seal, quite glad to dispense with all the hiding for once.

Sakura and Tomoyo burst into laughter, while Yukito and Xiaolang chided the living teddy bear. Tomoyo proceeded to record the whole party, which consisted mostly of Kero devouring every single saccharine molecule on the table.

When it was all gone, Kero bellowed at Eriol, "Oi! Scottie! Gimme more!"

Eriol scoffed incredulously. He snapped his fingers, and the table restored itself. Kero proceeded to frenzy about the table, while most others were content to enjoy the show.

Sakura finished her tea and pinched a few takoyaki balls. Eriol rested his hand on her shoulder and whispered, "Could we talk a moment, alone?"

The chaos stopped a moment as Sakura and Eriol rose from the table. Xiaolang expressed concern as they left, but remained on Sakura's insistence. Clearly, he still distrusted the Scotsman.

Eriol led Sakura into a room sparsely illuminated by twilight from a single window. The room had a complex magic circle inscribed into the floor, but was otherwise empty. The door locked behind them. Sakura started to feel nervous, and waited for Eriol to say something. He waltzed around the edge of the circle, eying its intricacies.

"You didn't ask me one important question," he said.

"You forgot to ask me why I said 'In your face, Clow.'"

Sakura recalled the moment, in which it sounded like Eriol had finally been relieved of a terrible burden.

"It sounded like you hate Clow," she said. "You called him a ruddy b-word."

Eriol's lips trembled as he nodded. "To be honest, this existence has been a nightmare." He ignored Sakura's concerned frown and continued. "I have had Clow Reed's memories unfold within my mind since before I could walk. It actually hurts to have his immense magical powers coursing through my body. Sometimes, I just can't take it. I've lost count of the number of times I thought about ending it all." He looked at her, tears nearing his eyes. "But I always knew, once you transformed the Cards, that you would be able to help me."

Sakura clutched her chest nervously. "You're not asking me to kill you, are you?"

"Oh, no!" exclaimed Eriol with a chuckle. "God, no! There're still lots of things I'd like to do. But there is something you can do for me that no one else can do." He walked toward her and held out his hand. She took it, and the moment his fingers touched hers, her mind flooded with visions.

There stood the man she knew as Clow, in his resplendent cloak bearing the symbols of the sun and moon. In his hands, he held the Book of Clow. With a snap of his fingers, the clasp sealed and he handed it to a faceless figure. The unknown person left with Clow's blessing, and took the book into the shadows.

Then Clow held up the same key that hung from Eriol's neck. To it, he said, "Our vow stands fulfilled, my friend ... One last spell."

The key became a staff, to which he uttered a soft prayer. Then, with a flourish, he struck it to the ground. His body disappeared in a blinding flash and a maelstrom of energy that slowly divided. Much of the bright, energetic wisps remained in a single sphere of light, while other parts of the whole drifted outward into a second sphere. Its light seemed far gentler, more controlled, and certainly steadier. It slowly drifted into the distance, and faded from sight.

The first sphere, turbulent and rowdy, blasted outward across the world and through time. It suddenly bolted downward through the atmosphere, as if riding on a shooting star, until it landed in the belly of a red-haired woman living in Aberdeen, Scotland.

Sakura opened her eyes and found herself looking at Eriol. She realised he had the same nose and eyes as the woman in her vision.

"That was me Ma," said Eriol. "I was given all of Clow's memory, magic, and the twisted aspects of his personality. The personality is fun, and the memories're pretty interestin', but the magic ..." He shook his head. "Ruddy reprobate!"

"I saw another soul," said Sakura. "Clow broke himself in two."

"Yeah," said Eriol. "That guy, wherever he is, got all of Clow's self-control and people skills. Pro'ly a lot of his intelligence too." He stepped into the centre of the circle. "Here's what I want, quine. I need you to split the magic between me and that other guy."

"How?" stammered Sakura. "He isn't here."

"This magic circle will be enough," said Eriol. "I designed it this way. All you have to do is utter the spell I just told you, and the other guy'll have half my powers."

"You didn't tell me any spell," said Sakura.

"Look again," said Eriol. Sakura was initially perplexed, but a new incantation echoed in her mind. Eriol grinned at her amazed glance. He motioned her to proceed. "If you'd be so kind, Sakura."

Sakura activated the Star Wand and held it up. She closed her eyes and played the incantation in her mind. In response to her wand, the magic circle began to glimmer. Eriol panted with a cocktail of excitement and utter terror.

Sakura recited:

> *Sun and Moon, Earth and Sky,*
> *Ye stand unbalanced, so see I.*
> *One soul made two, yet stand askew.*
> *Allotments be matched and remade anew.*

Eriol gasped, a look of ecstasy on his face. Filaments of energy wafted from his chest and flowed outward. As if blown by a gale-force wind, they promptly rushed to the window, squeezing their way through the seams and out into the night.

The circle stopped glowing, and Eriol crumpled to his knees. Sakura raced to his side.

"I'm fine," panted the boy. His grin widened and he threw his arms around her. "Thank you so much, Cardcaptor Sakura."

18 | Farewells

The next day, the school received the disappointing news: Eriol Lamperouge was going back to Scotland. Class chiefs across the school quickly organised farewell cards to present to the teacher, who had become quite popular during his brief tenure. Sakura, knowing the real reason for Eriol's departure, was less disheartened. She knew she'd stay in touch, especially if ever a magical incident were to occur.

That didn't stop her from showing up at his mansion that afternoon. At the request of the school, she carried a bundle of farewell cards, signed by every single student. Tomoyo carried another bundle with a forlorn smile, while Xiaolang begrudgingly carried the rest.

Eriol emerged from the front door, and beamed.

"Well, I didn't expect a goin' away present," he chirped.

Sakura waited until he had loaded his luggage into the waiting car. She then handed over the cards. "These ones won't do magic, but they'll certainly make you feel better."

Eriol grinned with delight as he studied the first Card. Every student in Sakura's class had signed it in various colours. The backside was decorated with technicolour glitter. Another class had decorated theirs with drawings of basketball players. "That one's from my class," said Xiaolang.

"Ya did good, laddie," said Eriol as he shook

Xiaolang's hand. The Chinese boy couldn't help but begrudge him a smile. "You get stronger, ya hear?" Eriol added. "Ya almost gave me a real run for me money yesterday."

"Any time you want a rematch," retorted Xiaolang.

Eriol turned to Tomoyo and gave her a big bear hug. "Ow, Miss Daidouji, I'm gonna subscribe to your channel and watch every one of your videos."

"Really?" exclaimed Tomoyo. "But they're all about Sakura."

"I gotta support such a talented lass, eh!" retorted Eriol. "By the way, since you're such a good tailor, how about makin' a suit for me? I'll email ya my ideas."

Tomoyo clutched her chest with excitement. "I would be honoured!" And she hugged him a second time.

Eriol finally reached Sakura. "Walk with me a moment."

Sakura strode alongside the Scotsman, a bit away from Xiaolang and Tomoyo. She wasn't sure what he planned to say, that they shouldn't hear, but decided to let him speak.

"It's kinda weird," said Eriol. "I'd dreamed about meetin' you and gettin' rid of Clow's magic for so long. But the burden's gone now. And I feel a little empty."

"Well, maybe you can find someone," said Sakura. "Find your own Number One. And have kids and teach those kids magic."

Eriol chortled. "Won't that be fun? There *is* someone back in Aberdeen I had me eye on." He took Sakura's hands and looked straight at her. He gave a warm smile and said, "I am so glad to have finally met you, Sakura. Not just for that spell. I have not had more fun in my entire life than here."

Sakura gripped his hands tightly. The realisation that he was leaving finally settled in, and she rubbed away mounting tears.

"Sorry, I'm just," she stammered. "I'm going to miss you, is all."

Eriol pulled her into an embrace and whispered, "Remember this feeling. It won't be long before something else happens." He pulled back to look at her again. "When it does, you'll find your Number One."

Sakura's eyes widened, but could not figure out what he was talking about. Eriol moved away and bade final farewell to the trio. He hopped into the car and drove away.

* * *

Halfway to the airport, Eriol saw Yukito standing beside the road. He pulled over to let the boy in. Yukito subsequently transformed into Yue, whose gaze carried across his vicious ire.

"Explain yourself, Clow," he barked.

"I explained plenty yesterday," said Eriol. "You and Yukito share a consciousness. Weren't you listening?"

"Why couldn't you just reincarnate and be our new Master anyway?" yelled Yue. His reptilian eyes reddened, puffing out against his pale visage. "Why did you leave me alone?"

"You weren't alone, Yue," said Eriol. "The Cards and Kerberus were with you. And now you have Sakura."

Yue snapped, "But she's not *you*, Clow!"

Eriol smirked. His brow knitted as he summoned the courage to speak.

"I am not Clow, Yue," he said. "My name is Eriol Lamperouge. I may have inherited part of Clow's being, but I am not him, and never will be." He reached over and stroked Yue's hair. "Clow is dead, and will not come back," he said, the words intended to convey absolute finality.

Yue sighed. He diverted his gaze, frustrated with his own inability to control his emotions. He tried to press against his rage with reason, but only one sentiment won the battle.

"It's not like I don't like the new Master," he muttered.

"She's a nice person with a good soul. She certainly spoils Kerberus as badly as you ... Clow did." There was still conflict in his gaze. It let Eriol know he was trying to talk himself both into and out of accepting reality.

"Tell ya what," said the Scotsman, throwing the boy a bone. "How about I give Yukito my details? If ever you want to reminisce, call me." Yue gazed at him hopefully. "Just, keep an eye on the time in Scotland, aye?"

Yukito left the car and bade Eriol farewell. While his other half still anguished in grief, Yukito felt a twinge of gratitude.

Were it not for you, Clow, I would not have met Touya.

* * *

Franklin returned home early from work. In his hand was a well-read newspaper, the front page reading 'Near-Fatal Air Crash Averted.' The subtitle mentioned something about a magic girl, but Franklin hardly took such stories seriously. He'd bought it merely for a laugh.

He checked the chores board. Sakura was on dinner duty, while Touya had the night off. He checked the messages on his phone, and saw one from Sakura that read, "Going to see off Eriol. Will be back to cook dinner."

Franklin chuckled at his daughter's use of the kiss smiley. Of course, he fully expected her to be late.

No reason I can't give her a head start, he thought as he headed for the kitchen.

He heard footsteps coming down the stairs and saw Touya plod into the dining room. He sensed the faint aroma of expensive men's perfume, and noted the nice sport jacket Touya had thrown on. His son rarely wore that jacket.

"You off, are you?" asked Franklin.

"Yeah, so I won't need dinner," said Touya.

"A date?" asked Franklin.

Touya stammered, "No, just hangin' with Yuki." He

turned to leave.

"So a date," concluded Franklin with a smirk. He fixated his eyes on his son, who turned slowly.

Touya started to speak. "Uh ... Look, I don't know what –"

Franklin cut him off with a raised finger. "Trust me, a father knows things." His smile widened. "Just remember ... he hurts you, I'll kill him."

Touya's jaw dropped, and he made a face like a fish out of water. Then, he raced forward and threw his arms around his father. He squeezed the man tightly.

"You'd better get going, Touya," said Franklin. "Don't stand him up."

Touya backed away, a big smile on his face. He pointed at Franklin and said, "You're the man!" Then he raced out the door with a skip in his step.

Franklin just chuckled, and headed back to the kitchen. As he pondered what to cook for dinner, another voice sounded.

"That's why I married you," said the voice. It was so familiar and wonderful, Franklin just assumed it was his own imagination. He looked up and smiled at the apparition that had spoken. He then did a double take, and looked again. Nadeshiko smiled at him warmly and said, "Hello, Franklin."

"Nadeshiko!" he stammered, wondering if he'd hit his head.

"You're not hallucinating," said the woman.

Franklin clutched his chest. "Am I dead?"

"Nope," giggled Nadeshiko.

"Then I'm sleeping," concluded Franklin.

"No," chided Nadeshiko.

"Clearly drunk," blurted Franklin.

Nadeshiko gripped his hands. And he could clearly feel her presence. She looked at him fixedly.

"I have been here all along," she said. "I've been waiting for this day."

"How is this possible?" whispered a mesmerised Franklin.

Nadeshiko smiled, having never been more proud. "Let's just say our daughter is a girl who makes things happen."

* * *

Life returned to normal after Eriol left.

Tomoyo, having no more chaotic magical events to film, took to scripting and choreographing new Cardcaptor videos. Kero often took breaks from his gaming to harangue her with ideas. He even suggested Xiaolang be included in the videos, albeit reluctantly.

Sakura moved past her sadness at Eriol's departure, and looked forward to the new videos. The notion of spending more time with Xiaolang always put a smile on her face. About two weeks after Eriol left, on the Friday, she approached Xiaolang as he was finishing cleaning duty.

"I was thinking we should show Tomoyo and Kero that club," she said. Her tone was almost mischievous, but she didn't realise it.

Xiaolang smiled with equal excitement. "We can go tomorrow night, if you'd like."

"Why not tonight?" asked Sakura.

"I've got a scheduled call with my parents tonight," said Xiaolang. He said it as if he were discussing a chore.

"Well then, family's more important," said Sakura. "Tomorrow night, it is."

The next day was a Saturday, giving Sakura time to pick an outfit to wear. She invited Touya and Yukito out as well, but her brother declined, citing previous engagements.

"Another part time job, eh?" she asked.

"Nah, Yuki and I are goin' somewhere," said Touya. Sakura chuckled at the hidden meaning. But that only made Touya retort, "Kaiju."

"I'm not a Kaiju!" returned the short-tempered girl.

Thereafter, Sakura spent her day in her room. The Reflect Card took on her mirror form, allowing her to see herself in various outfits. Kero, along with all the other Cards, offered helpful advice. Only Bloom took notice of how much effort she was putting in.

"If I recall, Master, you didn't go to nearly as much effort for Yukito," said the floral being.

"Oh, yeah, how d'ya know that, since ya were sleepin' and all," said Kero.

"Forest and Aqua told me," said Bloom.

"She is correct, Master," said Blade. "This is a lot of effort for the Lee boy."

Sakura grumbled, "I just want to make sure I look nice. That's all."

"Sure, it is," said Kero under his breath.

Sakura heard Franklin's voice call her. She came down stairs and saw Tomoyo standing at the front door. The girl wrung her hands as she failed to conceal her distress.

"Tomoyo, what's the matter?" asked Sakura.

"Sakura, I," Tomoyo stammered. "I'm so sorry. Lee is leaving for Hong Kong ... Today!"

In that instant, Sakura's heart froze. She didn't hear any of Tomoyo's words after that. Her legs gave out as utter grief and horror filled her. She couldn't remember feeling so awful. As Xiaolang's presence vanished from her heart, it left a hole so big she couldn't imagine how it could ever be mended.

"I can't believe this," she babbled. "Why is he going? He didn't even say goodbye!"

Franklin suddenly grabbed her hands and lifted her up from the floor.

"What're you doing, silly?" exclaimed her father. "Get over to his place before he leaves and tell him."

Tomoyo's eyes widened at Franklin's words, and she stepped forward.

"Yes! You must do that!" she yelled vehemently.

"Sakura, the look on your face right now is the same

one I had when your mother died," said Franklin. "She was my Number One and always will be. And when she left, it felt just like that!"

"Don't you see, Sakura?" cried Tomoyo, an extremely excited grin on her face. "Lee is your Number One. He's the one you love. And you can't just let him go!"

Sakura's gaze shifted as she tried to sort through the confused feelings in her mind. An image of Yukito, standing beside a crucifix in his house, burst through her mind and paralysed her.

"He mightn't like me like that," she stammered.

"He does," said Tomoyo flatly. "He told me at Tsukimine Shrine, just after we got back from Tokushima."

That was all Sakura needed. Every ounce of doubt blasted from her mind, and all that remained was the feeling of dancing with Xiaolang. Nothing had ever been clearer in her mind. Franklin and Tomoyo stood aside, but Sakura hesitated.

"Wait a minute, I need to get something," she said with bright, excited eyes. She raced up to her bedroom, rummaged through the bottom desk drawer, and found her pink hand-made shisa.

"What up, Sakura?" asked Kero.

Sakura faced him and proclaimed, "Xiaolang's leaving for Hong Kong. But I love him and I need to tell him before he goes."

Kero's eyes narrowed as he glared at her. With a harrumph, he crossed his arms and grumbled, "If you must." Sakura hugged him, and then raced out of the room. As Kero recovered from the assault, he shook his head. "Definitely different from Clow," he mumbled.

Sakura raced down stairs and brandished the shisa. "I'm going to give him this."

"Great idea," said Franklin.

Sakura turned to Tomoyo and embraced her. "Tomoyo, thanks for telling me about you." She kissed her friend's forehead, and then leapt out the door and down the street.

She sprinted for a few hundred metres before she heard Franklin yell, "Hey! Don't run! Fly!" Sakura stopped dead in her tracks and turned in amazement. "Come on! Fly! What's wrong with you?" bellowed Franklin.

Sakura eyed Tomoyo, who was equally shocked. But quite frankly it was refreshing to have one less person to tiptoe around. Sakura procured the Star Key and uttered her incantation. Franklin brandished a proud smile as the Star Wand appeared in his daughter's hands, and wings appeared on her back.

"Go on then!" barked her father.

Tomoyo joined in. "Get him!"

Together, they chanted, "Go! Go! Sakura!"

As if their chants were fuel to her engines, Sakura swivelled and sprinted. Her wings flapped and she began to soar. In an instant, she was a speck on the horizon.

Franklin and Tomoyo leaned on their knees to catch their breath. The girl could only glance at the father incredulously.

"A father knows things, Miss Daidouji," he panted.

Tomoyo shook her head in amazement. Straight away, she started to wonder about her own father, and whether he would know about her. In that instant, she recalled the words that had made her acknowledge Xiaolang as a fitting partner for her best friend.

You'd hope she knows, he had said.

Franklin calmed himself and invited her inside for a cup of tea. Tomoyo chose to remain outside a little longer. When Franklin disappeared into the house, Tomoyo took her phone from her pocket and dialled her mother.

"Mom, could I ask a favour?" she mumbled.

"Sure thing, dear," said her mother.

"Can you come home from work early tonight?" Tomoyo stammered. "I have something I need to tell you."

* * *

Xiaolang's apartment was empty and locked.

Sakura used her senses, augmented by the Cards, to scan for his signature. She sensed it, faintly, near the airport. She took flight, pouring every ounce of her energy into the Flight Card. But it wasn't fast enough. So she cast out Gale, who gave her a good solid kick. She shot through the skies across Tokyo, no longer caring if anyone saw her.

Tokyo Haneda came up fast. She dove downward toward the entrance and hit the ground running. Anyone who noticed her saw only a bright blur. She stood in the middle of the terminal, completely out of breath and mentally drained. She reached out feebly with her senses, searching desperately for Xiaolang's presence. But all she detected were the confused travellers staring at her.

Then Sakura felt it, only barely. She opened her eyes and looked through the crowd. Waiting in line at the security check-in stood Xiaolang. Her aching heart gave her a second wind and she raced through the crowd toward him.

"Xiaolang!" she yelled, drawing the boy's attention. When he saw her, he looked like a robber caught in the vault. At the same time, he was both overjoyed and saddened to see her. He moved out of the line and walked to meet her.

Sakura doubled over and panted profusely. She was clearly drained, and yet was of such a single mind that it hardly mattered. She reached into her pocket and held out her pink shisa.

"This is for you," she blurted. Her racing heart foiled her effort to say more.

Xiaolang smiled and accepted the figurine. Then he reached into his pocket and held out a green and yellow shisa figure.

"I made it to match our eye colours," he said. "But I couldn't think of a good time to give it to you."

Sakura took it with delicate hands, and stroked it gently. She glared up at him. "You were going to leave without saying goodbye."

"I'm sorry," he said softly. "You can kick me if it'll make you feel better." He instantly regretted it when Sakura's foot made contact with his shin. He managed to stand erect and face her.

Sakura drew a deep breath. "Xiaolang, I need to tell –"

He silenced her with a finger to her lips.

"Forget the big speech," he said as he hooked his hand under her chin. "Let's just do this."

Sakura inhaled sharply as his lips connected with hers. It was only a brush, and hardly anything approaching a mere peck. But it was gentle and thoughtful. He pulled away to gauge her reaction, but didn't get far before Sakura's lips pursued him. She pressed her lips firmly against his and savoured the contact. She threw her every ounce of awareness into memorising his touch, which was course and soft at the same time. Her heart fluttered with joy and she enveloped her arms around him.

The kiss lasted an eternity, if an eternity was how long it took for Sakura to suffocate. She finally pulled away to breathe, and rested her head against his chest.

"Why did we wait until the last minute?" she moaned.

Xiaolang stroked her hair and said, "Lots of things had to happen first, for both of us."

"But now it's over," mumbled Sakura.

Xiaolang cradled her cheek and looked at her.

"I'm coming back," he said resolutely. "I've decided, once and for all. I'll get a permanent residency and move here. Then we'll be together."

Sakura beamed with delight. "Promise?"

"What are you, twelve?" scoffed Xiaolang.

Sakura didn't bother talking, and kissed him again. She didn't care that people were watching and snapping pictures. None of that mattered. She had her Number One finally. And it didn't matter if they were going to be apart for a while. When he came back, they'd be together forever.

She eventually let him go, and stood there as he gave a final wave and disappeared behind the security gate. And even though she couldn't see him, she remained a moment longer. She gazed down at the Star Wand in her hand. Had it not been for that wand and those Cards, she would never have met Xiaolang. She might never have experienced the joy of finding her Number One.

Sakura gripped the wand tightly, recalling all the hardships and all the fun. And in the face of all that joy and pain, she couldn't help but laugh, and think, *Being Cardcaptor Sakura is awesome!*

Epilogue

Franklin flipped through the complex document resting on his lap. The courier beside him repeated that it was just a standard non-disclosure agreement. Nevertheless, he checked every ounce of fine print he could find. He eventually signed it, and handed it to the man.

The black, unmarked car pulled up to a tall building in a remote area. He didn't feel the need to stretch after such a long car ride. He had to hand it to whoever these people were, for making both the car and the aircraft so comfortable.

The last flight he'd taken to Australia had been a nightmare.

A team of agents led him through the sliding doors of the building. Like the exterior, the interior had little distinguishing marks, save for the hexagonal tile work on the floor.

A man in a long, silver jacket stood waiting for him by the elevator. The man held his hand out and said, "Thank you very much for coming, Doctor Avalon."

"It's Kinomoto, now," said Franklin.

"Not here, it isn't," said the man. "I am Commander Tristan Costable of the Alchemic Regiment. I am honoured to finally meet you."

Franklin frowned and wondered, *Alchemic Regiment?*

He then looked around at the bland building interior. The whole thing was a perplexing mystery – even more so than being visited by his dead wife, or his daughter's magical powers.

Costable dismissed the other agents and led Franklin into the elevator. The elevator descended deep below ground. The pair emerged into a wide corridor, pockmarked with workstations sporting what must have been state-of-the-art equipment. People in blue and grey uniforms scurried about, working intently on all manner of odd research.

"I take it you're some kind of top-secret research firm?" asked Franklin.

"More than that, Doctor Avalon," said Costable as he led the man into an adjacent room. The door slid closed and blocked out the din. "We are an organisation dedicated to the study of Alchemy in its purest form. In so doing, we are a barrier against those who would exploit its power for their own ends. We protect the world."

Franklin nodded pensively.

"I believe you on that," he said.

"Given what your daughter is capable of, I'm not surprised," said Costable. He drew Franklin's attention to a black box. The man ran his hands along it most reverently.

"Well then, you dragged me from home and flew me to another continent," said Franklin impatiently. "I assume you want me to study some occult chicanery."

Costable smiled. "No, mate. Only to make your dream come true." With a flourish, he opened the box and showed Franklin the contents.

The man's jaw dropped in amazement at the ornate rod of lustrous silver. He ran his hands over the artefact, brushing against the engraved symbols etched into its surface. A reflection of its form glimmered off his spectacles.

"It does exist," he gasped. "Where did you find it?"

"Right where you said it would be," said Costable. He looked apologetic. "We needed to keep it from those with nefarious purposes." He drew near to the mesmerised archaeologist. "We need you to study it, Doctor Avalon," he urged. "Only you can decipher the secret of the Silver Key. We need to know how it works. The fate of our world could depend on it."

Franklin glanced at the man, and worry overtook him. He looked back at the artefact, glistening under the office light. It was for this that he forsook so many years of his life. In pursuit of it, he missed his parents' funeral. He'd been disowned for his madness.

Finally, the focus of his life's work sat before him. Yet he couldn't help but wonder whether it was worth it.

I might end up alienating Sakura and Touya, he thought.

He glanced up at the figure standing across the desk from him. Costable couldn't see that figure, nor hear her. Thanks to Sakura, only Franklin had that privilege.

What should I do, Nadeshiko?

His wife's ghost nodded with an encouraging smile. That was all the permission he needed.

Franklin looked at Costable and said, "Let's get started then."

"Bravo!" exclaimed Costable.

About the Author

Craig Stephen Cooper grew up in Wollongong, New South Wales, Australia. At a young age, he quickly developed a flare for the dramatic, an obsession with various video games, and an aptitude for expressiveness.

In response to his desire to develop video games, his parents allowed him to study software engineering under a tutor while still in primary school. At the same time, he took dance lessons after school. He later decided drama was a path better suited to his love of storytelling, and studied speech and drama during high school.

While completing a Bachelor of Computer Engineering, he underwent practical and theory examinations for an Associate Diploma of Performance Art. During his Doctor of Philosophy in Telecommunications, he taught speech and drama to primary school children. As a member of the Fellowship of Australian Writers, he has presented workshops on storytelling and poetry, drawing on his speech and drama studies.

Cooper conceived of *The AXOM* Saga while on a train from Fukuoka to Nagasaki in Japan. Under encouragement from his friends, he wrote the stories with a passion to equal his first novel, *Final Flight of the Ranegr.*

He also dabbles in video game and mobile app development.

About the Illustrator

Tessa Eden grew up upon the shores of Australia's sunny beaches, frolicking in the sand and exploring the beautiful underwater world. Her father being a software engineer, and mother an illustrator, it was natural that she would grow to combine the two, becoming a digital artist. She now spends her days painting digitally, and creating 3D animations and CGI for animation studios in Sydney.

www.ingramcontent.com/pod-product-compliance
Lightning Source LLC
Chambersburg PA
CBHW030427120726
47903CB00003B/850